THE CALCULUS OF CHANGE

$$\int \frac{d\,\heartsuit}{\text{♂}+\text{♀}} = ?$$

THE CALCULUS OF CHANGE

JESSIE HILB

CLARION BOOKS

HOUGHTON MIFFLIN HARCOURT

BOSTON NEW YORK

Clarion Books
3 Park Avenue
New York, New York 10016

Clarion Books is an imprint of Houghton Mifflin Harcourt
Publishing Company.
hmhco.com

The text was set in Berling LT Std.

Library of Congress Cataloging-in-Publication Data

Names: Hilb, Jessie, author.
Title: The calculus of change / Jessie Hilb.
Description: Boston ; New York : Clarion Books/Houghton
Mifflin Harcourt, [2018] | Summary: Overweight and pretty,
high school senior Aden gets caught up in an exciting new
friendship that quickly turns into unreturned
love—at least on Aden's side—even while it helps her get closer
to her deceased mother's heritage.
Identifiers: LCCN 2016051394 | ISBN 9780544953338
(hardcover) Subjects: | CYAC: Self-acceptance—Fiction. |
Grief—Fiction. | Jews—United States—Fiction. |
Love—Fiction.
Classification: LCC PZ7.1.H548 Cal 2018 | DDC [Fic]—dc23
LC record available at https://lccn.loc.gov/2016051394

Manufactured in the United States of America
DOC 10 9 8 7 6 5 4 3 2 1
4500693300

For my mom

THE CALCULUS OF CHANGE

*I*mmediately I want him. Not because he has pierced ears. Not because he has unruly brown hair and gray-blue eyes. I want Tate Newman because he is wearing a two-toned blue handwoven yarmulke atop his head. It's like he's wearing a piece of his soul outside himself. I've been watching him for a few weeks now. We have math together, which is where I noticed the yarmulke. He's just returned from a summer trip to Israel with a big group of Jewish kids from Bentley. He's the only one in the group still wearing his yarmulke, and when I look at him, I see audacity and spirit, and I want those things in my life. I decide I want *him* in my life.

"Aden."

He says my name like we've talked a million times before.

"Tate."

I wonder if he can hear the nervous laughter behind my voice.

"Calculus," he says.

And I know exactly what he means.

"Calculus," I say.

So this is how we meet. We meet after school in the hallway of Bentley High over happenstance and a calculus problem.

He couldn't know that I have a secret passion for all things calculus. Calculus, as it has been described by our math teacher, "is the study of change." I like the idea of infinitesimal change. Small change in several steps makes sense to me because it feels like somehow I can control it. I am in charge of getting the numbers and symbols where they need to go. And though from start to finish it looks different on paper, I am really showing the tiniest shift. What I can't control in real life is the sudden, catastrophic change that often comes without steps or warning and makes life insufferably different. Like a dead mom. Calculus? Calculus is change I can wrap my head around.

"Aden."

He says it again. My name.

"Yes," I say, answering the question he hasn't asked yet. "I can help you with the calculus problem."

"Thank you," he says.

I'm smiling again, and I notice when he looks at me he cocks his head a little like he's trying to figure me out.

"What?" I say.

"Fast friends."

"Fast friends?"

I let myself laugh because I might explode if I don't.

"Yes," he says. "It's weird we've never met before. I think we're supposed to be friends."

Supposed to be.

"Okay," I say. "Then let's be friends."

"*Fast* friends."

"Whatever that means, Tate. Fast friends."

Talking to Tate is like swimming underwater. Everything silences, and it's just him and me. But I can't breathe.

"Talk after class tomorrow and we'll sort something out?"

I can't breathe but somehow I speak. "Looking forward to it."

He smiles.

I'm toast.

*M*arissa lies on my bed reading a magazine, her feet resting on my pillow, her long brown-auburn hair hanging off the side in its usual mess of waves. A half-eaten candy bar sits next to her. How can she do that? Eat only half.

I'm at my desk working on a four-part calculus problem. I have part one and half of part two completed, but I'm not in the zone.

"Oh my God," she says. "Turn it up. I love this song."

She's right. The music is good. Really good. Deep, gospel-like singing, severe drums, a choral background. It's rock and soul, emotional. I lose myself. First, it's the singer's voice pulling me into the music and out of my calculus homework. Then, the drums have me tapping my pencil on the desk, bobbing my head with the beat. Finally, the choral background kicks in with the crescendo. Colors, lights, feelings burst and swirl in me. I close my eyes and let the music swallow me. And then the song is over and I look at my half-finished calc problem.

"Because I can concentrate so much better with the music blaring?" I say. I look past Marissa where my guitar leans against the nightstand. I wonder if I could trim the song down and cover it with just the guitar. I'd have to change the key. Lower.

Marissa tracks my gaze and props her head in her hands. "Write anything good lately?"

"I'm almost finished with the song I played for you the other day. It's not right, though."

She sighs, and with a smile she says, "Ade. Always the perfectionist. I thought it was amazing."

"It's not amazing yet."

"It will be." Just like that, Marissa believes in me, unfailingly, ferociously.

I put my pencil down, hating that my calculus problem is half finished and I'll have to start from scratch when I get back to it. But I should have known I wouldn't get much done with Marissa here. She flips the page in her magazine, a history book lying untouched on the floor next to her.

"Make contact with Josh today?" I ask her.

"Yeah."

"And?"

"And he's so . . . uninteresting."

"Uninteresting?"

"I'm bored. We have to stop doing our thing. It's so old."

I think about Josh and his piercings and his attitude and the way he's always just *there* for Marissa, and I say, "Yeah.

I get it." I feel bad for the guy. Josh pales in comparison to Marissa, with her light and love and charisma. He's a stoner who fails classes and plays video games every spare second. But he's been home base for Marissa all through high school. He's the guy she'll keep returning to because he's a warm body, and he always wants her. The same cannot be said of her deadbeat dad who left when she was a little girl.

"So who now?"

She raises an eyebrow and glances back at her magazine.

"Missy! Who?" She hates it when people call her Missy, but I do it because we've been best friends since forever ago.

"Lance," she says, still looking down.

"Lance? Lance who?"

"Lance Danson."

"Wait, what? I'm confused." Mr. Danson is an English teacher at our high school. A shaggy-haired, white-button-up-shirt-wearing English teacher with muscular forearms. He incites passion in his students because he cares so much. I had him for English last year.

"His name is Lance Danson," she says slowly, enunciating every syllable.

"As in *Mr.* Danson?"

She looks up without raising her chin, her eyes hooded so I can't read her expression.

"Huh. Mr. Lance Danson. Seriously? You have a thing for a teacher?"

She rolls onto her back, looking at me upside down. "I don't know. It's complicated."

"I'll bet it's complicated. He's, like, a thousand years old."

"You know he's not." It's true. I know he's only twenty-six or twenty-seven.

"He said I have the eyes of an angel."

I choke a little on the soda I've been sipping. "He didn't."

Marissa smiles and pulls the hair tie out of her hair.

"When did Danson talk to you about your eyes?" I say.

"When I stayed after school yesterday to work on my essay."

"Huh. Weird."

"Why is that weird? You don't think I have beautiful eyes?" She flutters her eyelashes at me and puckers her lips. I roll my eyes. In fact, I do think she has beautiful eyes.

I throw my pencil at her.

"Dude. Don't throw shit at me." She tosses the pencil back and it hits the wall, bouncing off so that I have to duck.

I toss my hands up in surrender.

"So you were just, like, what? Leaning over the desk under the guise of working on your essay, and he looks up into those bad boys of yours and says 'Oh, Marissa, you have the eyes of an angel'?"

Marissa laughs. "Something like that, cheese ball."

"Wow."

I think about Danson and his arms and smile and the way he paces the room when he's onto an idea. And I understand the attraction there. I do. It seems weird that Danson would tell Marissa she has *angel eyes*. I wonder if she took it out of context. Either way, Marissa changes love interests daily. I'm sure this will pass.

"Dude," I say because something niggles at the back of my mind anyway, "be careful there."

She laughs. "Careful is my middle name." *Careful* is far from how I'd describe my best friend.

She goes back to her magazine, perusing the story with the title "I Was in a Relationship with (insert celeb-of-the-week name here)!" She's not vapid. I've heard some of the girls in my AP English class talking about her. I'm sure they were speaking out of jealousy, or if Marissa got to one of their boyfriends. I believe the word they used was *vacuous*. As though a single one of them has any clue about Marissa. I know her. She's a mess. She's wild. She spontaneous. She's funny. She's desperate for male attention, and she knows exactly what to do to get it. She's directionless. But she's my best friend, and I love her not in spite of all that, but in part because of it.

"Your turn," Marissa says. "Spill."

I guess we're done talking about Danson and angel eyes. Which is okay because it weirds me out to think about Danson like that. He's one of my favorite teachers.

"Spill what?"

"There's something we're not talking about. I haven't heard a word about what's-his-name."

"Cody. His name is Cody."

"Are we still crushing or have we moved on?"

"I believe we've moved on." I can't think of Tate without that stupid smile. A dead giveaway.

Cody is the senior class's best-looking lacrosse player. He's also been in my brother's circle of friends for the last three years. He's completely unattainable. He's nice enough, but I know he doesn't see me *in that way*. I've been crushing on him for a long time, but somewhere in me I must know it's not going to happen. Plus, besides his wonderful looks and the fact that he's sweet, Cody doesn't seem . . . thoughtful. Like Tate. Or electric, like Tate.

Marissa turns her attention back to the magazine. She takes another agonizingly slow and small bite of the candy bar. Now she's on the "Spotted at the Beach!" section of the magazine, one skinny movie star after another clad in nothing but strings. I have the sudden urge to rip the candy bar away from her and scarf the rest in one huge, satisfying bite because, my God, I will never be skinny and I'm so sick of wanting it.

She's impassive when she says, "Who is he? Do I know him?"

"I'm not sure." I sigh. Out with it. "Tate Newman?"

She pauses, scanning her brain. "Nope. I don't think I do. Senior?"

"Yeah. Yarmulke."

"What?"

"He wears that yarmulke around. You know, the little hat that Jewish guys wear."

"Oh yeah. That." She looks up. "He wears one to school? Seriously?"

"Yes, seriously."

"Why?"

"I don't know. I guess it means something to him."

"Huh. And you like him?"

"Kinda." Understatement of the week. "It's cool he wears the yarmulke. Different. He has earrings, too. I like it."

"Huh," she says again. "So do you think he's into you?"

I guess I hadn't fathomed the possibility.

"Don't know." I'm trying to sound casual when it's so far from what I feel. Giddy, awkward, sparkly. But casual and cool? Not me right now, or ever, really.

TATE

I lean against a locker on the other side of the hall, opposite Tate, watching him. He's talking to a group of kids. I'm etching in my mind the way he throws his head back and laughs when someone says something funny. I want to make him laugh like that. He's completely unselfconscious. No one wants to miss a beat of what Tate says because he's fluorescent in an otherwise dull, lightless room. He thinks no one is watching, or maybe he doesn't care. But I'm watching. I think everyone in his general proximity is watching—at least out of the corner of an eye. He's a glow stick.

He looks up from the conversation and smiles. At me. I guess he knows I've just been stalking him. I lift my hand in a half wave, and I think a full-on bird just flew out of my mouth because butterflies-in-my-stomach doesn't begin to describe what happened to my body when Tate smiled.

"Problem number three," he says.

We're both smiling stupidly. As if problem number three is some inside joke between the two of us, when really it's just a math problem that at least forty other kids were tasked to solve.

"I know," I say. "Did you figure it out?"

"I needed you."

I can't get my mouth out of this smile.

"Everyone needs me." Still smiling.

I might be trying too hard. Am I trying too hard? I wish I hadn't said *that* of all things.

He laughs. I just made Tate laugh.

Then neither of us says anything for a beat. Laughing gray-blue eyes are my new drug of choice.

"My dad doesn't know I have a C," Tate says.

"In math?"

"Yeah. He wants me to be a doctor or an engineer. Like him."

"Your dad's a doctor?"

"Yeah. Neurosurgeon."

"Jeez. No pressure."

"Ha. I know, right?"

He looks so weary. I feel like hugging him because I can't seem to stand close enough. But we're in the hallway of Bentley High between classes and this is only the second time we've talked. I concentrate on breathing for a half second because I could swear I've forgotten how.

Instead I reach out and touch his arm.

"I'm sure you don't suck at it."

He doesn't seem to notice that my hand was on his arm for far too long.

"Would you be willing to help me? Like forever?"

I want Tate to say the word *forever* to me again and again and again.

He laughs a little, the sound bouncing off the walls in my head, a low, clear brass instrument—a tenor sax.

"Obviously, yes."

I just said that out loud when I meant to say *yes*.

"Okay, then. After school?"

"Sure. I'll meet you at the benches."

The benches are an area where only seniors are allowed at Bentley. One of those unspoken rules. I rarely go there because I think people who feel particularly cool hang out there and I've never felt particularly cool. But today I throw caution to the wind. Today I crash the dreaded benches.

Tate raises an eyebrow.

I laugh. He caught me. Am I see-through?

"We meet there. We walk to Ike's," I say.

"Okay. I'll buy the coffee."

"Deal, but I only drink coffee if it's a mocha," I say.

He laughs. I just made Tate laugh again, and I could listen to that sound on repeat. If I had a pen and paper, I could write a song to the sound. It's not high-pitched, but not low or booming. He laughs in D-minor.

"A mocha is not coffee. It's a hot milkshake."

"Great, then you can buy me a hot milkshake."

"See you at the benches," he says.

* * *

I have to remind myself that today I'm a senior and I'm meeting Tate Newman at the place where everyone at Bentley who matters hangs out, and this is all okay because talking to Tate about nothing makes me feel like something. And no one cares where I happen to meet new friends.

I stand next to a group of kids I've probably never talked to in all of our school years together. As I watch the girls around me, I'm conscious that I'm not wearing a chic pair of knee-high leather boots. Likely because I can't get a pair of leather boots to zip over my calves. They're the cool kids. I've never been a cool kid. What was I thinking, meeting him here?

I breathe and sit down. I question my decision to sit down as soon as I do it. Cross a leg. Uncross the leg. Look down at my thighs and cross a leg again. Repeat. Try not to think about my thighs or my calves or some other part of my body that would disqualify me from wearing what I want. Where the hell is he? It's been fifteen minutes since the bell rang, and on the day I finally decide to the brave the benches, Tate *would* forget. Or worse, decide he had something better to do than hang out with me and a calculus problem. I scan the crowd for someone I know, but then a girl with long blond hair — Stacey? — moves, and I see Tate.

He's surrounded by another group, again with the energy and the lit-up face and the attention of everyone in this general area. I forget what I was thinking because thinking isn't something I can do when Tate makes everything in me vibrate. And that's before he looks at me.

He's midsentence when he spots me sitting on the bench, watching him, legs crossed. His smile suspends time. He waves me over, and I am not my calves or my thighs or my awkward legs crossed, because Tate sees me.

"Guys, this is Aden, the girl I was telling you about. Calculus wiz, and she's awesome, too."

I laugh.

With Tate stands a freckled, redheaded girl I've never seen and Paul and Alana, friends of mine. I smile at the redheaded girl and immediately forget what Tate said her name was. I didn't realize Tate and I had mutual friends. This fuzzy, fluffy, bird-in-my-stomach thing is happening and the stupid smile, and I wonder if everyone can see it. I feel transparent.

"We know Aden." Paul elbows my arm with familiarity. I smile and nudge back, glancing at Tate. He raises an eyebrow in surprise, those gray blues vibrant, interested. Surprising Tate just became my favorite thing.

"You all know each other?" Tate says.

"We do." I amaze myself with the ability to speak because my body and mind are saying everything should be to the contrary.

"Yeah," says Alana. "It's the choir thing. We're tight." Alana winks at me.

"Awesome," Tate says. We look from each other to Tate. "I love it when cool people know each other."

I can't focus on anything other than Tate and the space he consumes, a universe.

"We have a bitch of a calculus problem to solve," he says.

He puts a hand on my shoulder, pointing me in the direction of Ike's.

I disintegrate.

* * *

I concentrate on the sounds our feet make as we walk side by side to Ike's—it makes me feel sane. Otherwise I'd lose myself when Tate is next to me, and I'd end up saying something embarrassing and not sane. Four feet walking forward. The sound is soft on grass, and then there's the crunch of the first autumn leaves underfoot. Louder on concrete. Like the sound of bongos and then the clash of symbols. We make eye contact. Tate's eyes are filled with a kind of wonder, and suddenly there's this word on the tip of my tongue . . . *hope*.

He holds the door open for me, motioning for me to go ahead. I squint up at him.

"I'm perfectly capable of opening a door," I say.

"Prove it." He steps aside and the door slams shut while the two of us stand there staring at it.

I push him to the side with my hip and grab the door handle.

A man behind us clears his throat before Tate makes a big deal out of walking through the doorway.

"Thank you," Tate says. "This is so kind."

I roll my eyes and continue holding the door for the man behind us.

"Yes," says the man. "Thank you." I can't tell if he's annoyed or joking.

Then Tate reaches around the stranger and grabs my hand, pulling me into line with him, into him. I glance at the man, hoping he sees the apology on my face.

As we stand in line together, Tate puts a hand on my back, between my shoulder blades, inching me forward. My skin burns in the best way underneath his hand.

The barista looks from me to Tate.

"A small mocha, please." I take the lead.

"Whip?" He writes some kind of symbol on the cup.

"Obviously," I say to the barista with a smile.

Tate elbows me. "Thatta girl."

"Glad you approve."

"Approve? Nah. I totally worship you."

"Wow. All it takes is whipped cream? You must be easy."

"You have no idea," he says with a wink.

This feels like flirting, and I'm on fire, and how do people do this—flirt—when everything inside feels ablaze?

I want to say something witty, but I can't speak or breathe or function. His hand is still there, a torch between my shoulder blades, a slow, sweet burn.

Tate pays for both of our drinks. "You better make this mocha worth my while," he says as he removes his hand from my back.

"I'm sure I already have."

We sit in the corner next to the window.

"So you're a genius, right?" Tate is pulling his math book out of his backpack.

"Yes, but I'm not doing this *for* you."

"I'd never ask you to," he says without irony. "But I can't get a C in this class."

"Because of college?"

"That and my dad."

"Pressure?"

"Well, I've spent the last eighteen years tricking him into thinking I'm smart, like him."

"But you're not?"

When he smiles at me, it doesn't reach his eyes. "Not in the way he thinks."

"What does that mean?"

He runs a hand through his curly brown hair. "I don't know. I'm a lost cause."

"I don't get it. Why?"

"I hate math," he says.

"So? You don't have to love math, or even be good at it, to be smart."

"Yeah."

"So why is math so important to your dad?"

"Math and science. All of my grades, really. I think it's the whole neurosurgeon thing."

"Oh."

"It's not like he expects me to be a doctor, but he thinks I'm an idiot because of what I want to be."

"Well, what do you want to be?"

"A musician."

I raise an eyebrow. "Really?"

"Yeah."

"Cool."

I have this vision of Tate and me playing music together, and it's so powerful I look at Tate and wonder if he can see my thoughts.

Tate stares down at his coffee cup, turning it in circles, his mind lost in his dad's unfulfilled expectations.

"Your dad wants you to have more security in life."

"I guess. But it's like he's asking me to be someone I'm not."

"Yeah, it sucks to feel like you're letting him down."

"Yeah." He looks up for just a minute, and when our eyes meet, something I can't name passes between us. It's more than understanding; it's recognition. We both know what it means to live up to impossible standards. Even if no one says it out loud, I carry so much weight for my family—the weight of my dad's unresolved grief and the weight of my brother's everything. And Tate, having to be someone he's not to make his dad proud. I get it.

"So what do you play?" I say.

"What?"

"You want to be a musician: what instrument do you play?"

"Piano. I play the piano."

"Really? Classical?"

"Jazz, mostly. But I can play bits of anything."

"Do you sing, too?" I ask. We could play an epic duet.

"Hell, no. I can't carry a tune to save my life."

"I can."

"Oh yeah?"

I answer him with a smile, too hypnotized by the fantasy of us onstage together to say anything else. Tate on piano, me singing with my guitar, bright stage lights, the two of us imbued with our music.

"I'd love to hear you sing sometime."

Love.

"Sure." My answer is *sure* out loud, when, really, the answer is something more like *I'll sing to you and in you and with you and about you.*

"So what about you?" he says. "What do you want to be?"

"Like, when I grow up?"

He laughs.

"Because, isn't that pretty much tomorrow?" I say.

"Or a few months. Or years."

"I don't know. I want to be a math major."

"Figures."

I stick my tongue out at him.

"I might double in music composition. But only if I can find a program that will support the kind of song writing I love."

"Which is what?"

"Mostly folk and rock."

"Where are you applying?" He takes a drink of his latte.

A piece of curly hair falls into his eyes. I wish I could lean forward and brush it away.

"NYU, Brandeis, and CU."

"Top choice?"

"I think it's Brandeis."

"Really? You know that's a Jewish school, right?"

"In fact, I do, Mr. Jewish." I wink at him.

"So what's the draw?"

"Um." I pause. "My mom went there. She's Jewish, and she—" I don't know why I just talked about my mom in the present tense. It feels easier than dropping the casual she-died bomb on him right now.

"Really? You know, officially, that makes you Jewish, too?"

"I know," I say. "But I wasn't raised that way or anything. So I don't feel Jewish."

"Well, maybe you just need to find a way to connect with it."

"How?"

"Take a trip to Israel."

"Ha. Yeah, right."

"Seriously, you should look into it. It's called Birthright. You can get a fully funded trip. Find out who you are, Aden."

"I know who I am, Tate."

Tate leans back in his chair, and I swear I could jump into his smile and stay in its warmth forever.

MOM

There are three pictures of my mom in the house. One is of her hugely pregnant with me, on a bicycle. It's in a frame on my dad's nightstand. When I want to stare at that one, I have to make sure he's not home. I know my dad looks at that picture every night before falling asleep, because each morning I find it face-down in his bed and I set it back on the nightstand. It's been a strange, unspoken ritual between us for years. In the mornings when Jon and I get up for school, my dad is already downstairs eating toast and drinking coffee. So I get ready in Dad's bathroom and Jon uses ours.

A few years ago it started bugging me that his bed was always unmade. Especially because my dad is so particular about the way we park our car and where we store the TV's remote control. It seemed out of character. My mom used to make the bed and throw decorative pillows on it every morning. None of the pillows matched, and it drove my dad crazy. All the plaids, stripes, and solids converging on their bed. My mom would laugh at my dad's uptight need to have everything color coordinated and neutral, and he, in turn, laughed at her need for vibrancy. After she died I never once saw their bed made, and I don't know what my dad did with my mom's pillows. So I started straightening their bed, which was when I found her picture buried in the blankets.

When I turned the picture over and saw my mom's joyful face a little swollen with pregnancy staring back at me, all the wind rushed out of my lungs. She's squinting into the sun, hand shielding her eyes, her awkward bike helmet small in comparison to the size of her belly. I've looked at the picture so often, half the time I think of her, I see her pregnant on a bicycle.

The other two pictures hang on the wall leading to our basement, and they're part of picture collages. In one she's kissing me at my kindergarten graduation. Her hair is a fluffy brown mess of curls that fall over both our faces. My cheeks are unnaturally pink. I remember begging her to let me wear makeup as I watched her get ready in the morning. She laughed and said that I could wear a little blush *just this once* because it was my *special day*. In the other picture she and my brother are casting a fishing rod into a river together. Their hands are intertwined over the rod, and they're both laughing. My mom has a brown vest on with bright orange feathers peeking out from the many pockets.

I think she loved being a mom. The mom I see in my memories is so fogged up with the few pictures we have of her in the house. I *think* I remember the camping trip where she and my brother are fishing, but I'm not sure. I know I can't remember when she was pregnant with me on a bicycle, but it's as though I can.

I hate that my memories of her are fading, replaced by moments in time that I don't know if I remember. I hate that the essence of her is trickling out of me day by day, year by year. The older I get, the farther away she is. So often I wonder, *What would my mom have said or done?* She would've kissed my blushed cheek, laughed with her head thrown back while holding a fishing rod, or waved at me with a pregnant belly from her bicycle. I try to believe that she's somewhere, that she's more than the still life in those three pictures, that her spirit hasn't ceased to exist, but I can't make her show up for me when I need her.

TATE

There's a small mocha and a large latte on the table between the two of us. The latte must be the size of my face, and if Tate weren't so tall, I probably wouldn't be able to see him over the top of it. I keep my head down, trying so hard not to get swept away in the current pulling me toward him. But when I'm with Tate, everything is more alive—not like fireworks, like a thousand buzzing Christmas bulbs, a low hum, the colors all twinkly.

I sit tall, peering over the latte, teasing him about the monstrous size of his coffee.

"I know," he says. "It's one of my vices. Large lattes and sour candy. Lots of sour, lots of candy, copious amounts of caffeine. Lots of peeing."

I laugh. He pulls a pack of Sour Patch Kids out of his backpack and tosses it on the table.

"Help yourself," he says.

"Thanks." I help myself to a handful.

It's a little early for Sour Patch Kids—third period—but I'm not one to turn down candy.

Liz Weedle walks by our table. She waves at Tate. She's wearing Converses, skinny jeans, and a cardigan set. She's boyish but cute. Unquestionably thin. Tate gazes after her as she walks away. I cross one leg over the other. I wonder if she eats.

"She's kind of beautiful, right?" Tate says.

"What?"

"Liz. You're staring."

"I guess," I say. "I mean, I am staring. You think so? Beautiful, I mean?"

"There's something about her."

"Like what?"

"I don't know," he says. "It's in her body. The way she carries herself."

"How does she carry herself?"

He smiles and twirls the mechanical pencil he's holding. "I don't know. Kind of like a bird."

His answer surprises me. I'm not sure what I was expecting him to say, but it certainly wasn't something about a bird.

"A bird?"

"Yeah." He takes a drink, twirls his pencil. "I guess it's also her sharp features. But the way she walks. It's like she's weightless."

"What's so great about being weightless?"

"Freedom."

His smile is all mischief and come-hither.

I sigh. I wonder what freedom feels like.

I've already finished the calculus homework, so I open my scribble notebook where I write ideas for song progressions and lyrics. I rework the verse I wrote yesterday, studying the new arrangement carefully, and when I look up, Tate is staring at me. Our eyes meet, and I'm lost in the warmth just before he smiles; I see light and no judgment, and I'm a puddle on the table soaking our drinks and Sour Patch Kids.

I watch as he erases the same set of numbers on his worksheet for the third time in a row.

I put my finger on the paper next to the numbers and symbols. "You can't move the Y over before you solve Y plus P," I say.

"Oh. Right." He starts to solve the problem and then throws his pencil onto the table. "I need a break."

I wonder how he can need a break right now, when he's so close to stumbling on the solution.

"Do you ever just drive?" he says.

"Sometimes. Come on, keep going. Don't you see? You're almost there." I point to the numbers on his worksheet.

"Eh." He says it like it just doesn't matter, and I can't imagine how he can look at those symbols and numbers without needing them to make sense. But in a way I guess it's liberating—just throw the pencil down and walk away.

"We're going for a drive."

"We've only been here for fifteen minutes," I protest.

"And that's fifteen too long of me not figuring out this calc problem."

"But you *are* figuring it out."

"Good," he says. "Then when I come back to it, it won't be so hard."

"That's not how it works."

"Can we take your car?"

He's standing now, his hand pressed lightly into my shoulder blades, nudging me out of my seat. I think I'm about to walk away from an unsolved calculus problem, which is totally sacrilege for me.

"You're gonna forget what you were doing with that problem. Don't say I didn't warn you." I'm smiling and shoving things into my backpack. "And we'll never make it back for fourth."

"We will," he says. "A short drive. Let's say seven songs' worth."

"Seven? That could be half an hour, depending on the songs. And we need time to park."

"Fine. Six. No more arguing."

***

We're driving and the wind is whipping my hair around my face and Tate leans his head back in the passenger seat, one hand out the window like a little kid. It's not long before we're out of town. Vast yellow plains meet soaring wispy clouds that jut right up against the Western Slope, which is a mountainous breadth, a god.

I lean forward and turn the music down. The wind is still loud, and I have to raise my voice to be heard.

"So why the yarmulke?"

"What?"

I reach my hand over and touch the top of his head where the yarmulke starts. "The yarmulke."

He turns and looks at me, his mouth pinched. His mouth. It's the shape of a heart. I bet it would fit against mine.

I think he's trying to decide if he can trust me.

I roll up the windows

"Sorry if I'm prying. It's just that I like it."

"You do?"

I nod.

"Why?"

"You first," I say. "Why do you wear it?"

"I wear it because it's a symbol of what happened to me in Israel this summer and because it reminds me who I am."

"I have more questions."

What "happened" to him in Israel? The way he says it —it obviously wasn't a traumatic experience. My friend Becca went on the same trip last year, and when she came back, she claimed she'd been "transformed." She told of sleeping in tents and waking at sunrise and visiting holy sites. As she spoke, I pictured orange light cast over sandy brown desert. Campfires and song. Deep conversations under an unpolluted sky full of stars and moon. Was all of that transformative or just really fun?

"I'm sure you do have questions," he says. "But now you. What do you like about the yarmulke?"

"The colors."

He laughs.

"Okay, fine. I like it because I think it means you're moved."

"What do you mean, *moved*?"

"I mean you're somehow more inspired, more impacted, more . . ." I pause, searching for the right word, feeling my cheeks burn hot as I realize how much I'm giving away.

Tate smiles before I find the word. "I was." He takes a drink of his giant latte. "Moved."

"Shouldn't *moved* be a constant state of being?"

"That sounds intense and exhausting, Ade."

I'm lost in the way he uses my favorite nickname.

"It's better than the alternative."

"Which is what?"

"Something like death, I guess," I say.

Tate reaches for my hand and interlaces our fingers. It feels like being held from the inside out. I wish this feeling, this moment, would last forever.

JON

*J*on is standing in the entrance of my bedroom, tapping lightly on the open door. I look up from my math homework and wave him inside. He wanders in, hands in his pockets, and sits on the edge of my bed. He reminds me of a seven-year-old. He has the same thick ruffle of unruly hair as me. His jeans are a comical mix of tight and loose, sagging in the waist but tight through his hamstrings, as is all the rage. He's wearing an equally tight T-shirt with robots printed on the front. I think he's making *dork* look cool. He can do that. He's a crossover. Everyone likes him because he makes people laugh. He has friends in every subgroup and seems mostly unaware of the social caste system at Bentley. I guess being his sister gives me a few ins I wouldn't otherwise have.

"What's up?" I say.

"Nothing."

So it's going to be like talking to a seven-year-old.

"Jon?"

I wait quietly.

He sighs. "A girl."

"Ah. Who?"

"You don't know her. She's a sophomore."

"Try me."

"Sabita Patel?"

"Sabita. Beautiful name. But nope, don't know her. So what's the deal?"

"I like her."

Jon and I have always told each other about relationships or love interests. Maybe it's because we don't have a mom. Well, he tells me about relationships, I tell him about love interests. He's had girlfriends since middle school. I've never had a boyfriend.

"That's great."

"She's really pretty."

"Oh," I say.

She's pretty. I'm trying not to let my reaction to the word *pretty* get in the way of this conversation. What is it about that word? Maybe it's because I'm always wondering if I'm pretty. Sometimes it feels like pretty is all that matters. And in my reality, *pretty* is synonymous with *thin*. She must be thin. I've never seen Jon date a girl who isn't.

"What does she look like?"

"She's Indian. She has this incredible, long black hair. And her eyes, and, well. This is embarrassing, Ade. Jeez. You'll just have to meet her, okay?"

"So did you come here to tell me about how pretty your new girlfriend is or is there something I can help you with?" I know I sound bitter, but I can't think about pretty and what it means and how I stack up without wanting to detonate. It's too much pressure, too many standards, and it's all bullshit.

"Well, could a sister help a brother figure out what to do on our first date?"

I laugh.

"Yes," I say. "I believe I could."

I wonder if he'd be talking to my mom about this instead of me if she were alive. Missing her always hits like this. In the middle of something. Like a sudden blow to the gut. Missing her for my brother is excruciating. As though I don't miss her enough for myself. Jon doesn't get a mom. Every little boy needs a mom.

"Well, what does she like to do?"

"She's an artist."

"Cool. What kind of art?"

"A sculptor. I guess she takes pottery, but she stays after school every day and works on these clay sculptures."

"Easy. Art museum."

"I mean, I know she likes art. But I can't think of something that says *trying too hard* like the art museum. Plus it's boring. Try again."

"Okay. Arthouse film."

"Closer. But also boring."

"Paintballing?"

"Yeah. Something like that."

"I'm pretty sure you didn't need me to come up with an idea like paintballing."

"I always need my big sis."

Jon is only eleven months younger than me, but I've always been the big sister. He jokes that his favorite month of the year is February, not because it's his birthday month but because he's the same age as me every February. He says I don't get to boss him around in February. Which is stupid because I have every right to boss him around whenever I please.

TATE

"*M*aggie Tiley," he says.

"I'm sorry, what?"

"I was just saying that at some point this weekend I'll hang out at Maggie's."

Tate saying the name Maggie Tiley isn't making sense to me. They don't strike me as kids who would travel in the same social circle.

"Oh. I didn't know you guys knew each other."

"Yeah. We're, um, together."

"Oh."

I think I've already said *oh*. "Cool."

But it's so far from cool. It's a knife. "How long?"

Did I just vomit a bunch of Sour Patch Kids all over the table?

"What?"

"How long have you guys been together?"

"Oh. Six months."

"Oh."

Of course it would be Maggie Tiley. With her long

golden hair and sun-kissed freckles. With her thin. It would have to be Maggie Tiley. Maggie who gets the solos in choir. Maggie who once had a crush on my brother and befriended me to get close to him. Maggie who dropped me when she dropped her crush on my brother. I feel a stab of humiliation as I realize how stupid I've been. I had thought maybe Tate could like me.

"You didn't know I had a girlfriend."

"You didn't mention it."

"Yeah," he says, "I guess I didn't. It never really came up."

"I know Maggie."

"Oh yeah? That doesn't surprise me." He pauses. "She knows most of the singer-theater types."

"Yep," I say. "We travel in the same circles. She's supposed to be a part of this organizing committee we have for open mic night here at Ike's, but she hasn't made the meetings yet."

"You need a committee for that?"

I throw a Sour Patch Kid at him.

"Yes. We have to figure out sound and get an MC, and we need to have an idea of who's performing. It's not that involved, but yeah, it takes a little planning. And then we have to spread the word."

"So what's the word? When is the next one?"

"Last Friday of every month. So, three and half weeks?"

"Are you singing?"

"I am. Are you coming?"

"I am now," he says.

It hits me like a promise and I forget that he just told me that Maggie Tiley is his girlfriend. I feel just a little lighter.

MR. DANSON

*P*assing period. Seven minutes every forty-nine minutes, and it's impossible to gather your books and make it from one end of the biggest high school campus in the history of campuses to the other end, unless you wheel a suitcase around. Some kids do. I'm not there yet—I have some pride. But I might as well buy a suitcase. My pack is stuffed to the brim, and I'm carrying not one, but two fifteen-pound books as I haul ass from the south building to the north building.

I think about what I can accomplish in exactly seven minutes. Pee and wash my hands, maybe. If there isn't a line. Solve a quarter of a math problem. Eat a delicious, addictive, half-baked chocolate chip cookie from the school cafeteria. But sift my way through a crowd of chattering teenagers for a mile? In seven minutes? *No.*

I round the corner right into Mr. Danson. I think of English last year and how he'd gesture wildly *and* do voices when reading Shakespeare aloud.

"Ade!"

Danson uses my nickname, and in any other circumstance

I wouldn't have noticed, but now I'm picturing him and Marissa and something cheesy like angel eyes, and did I just make eye contact? With his crotch? I curse Marissa for getting into my head like this.

"Danson. I mean, Mr. Danson."

At least I didn't call him Lance.

"How is AP literature going this year? You have Cammie Misley, right?"

Yet another first name of a teacher I did not need to know.

"I do. It's good, thanks."

"I hear she's a hard-ass."

"She's okay. Probably one of my better teachers this year."

"That's because you don't have me."

It's easy to see how his interactions could feel just over the edge of friendly—flirty. But *eyes of an angel?*

Being the object of Danson's attention is momentarily intoxicating, and I find myself thinking like Marissa. He's wearing a royal blue button-down, sleeves rolled halfway up his ripped forearms. And his hands—

The bell. I'm late.

*S*o you're saying Y is a function of X?"

I laugh. He wasn't lying about math: it's not his thing.

"No, I'm saying Y_1 equals Y plus P."

We're sitting across from each other, and I'm trying so hard not to solve the problem for Tate.

I go back to writing lyrics in my notebook.

What is beauty
but something that's here
and then gone, like everything?

Tate stops me every few minutes to ask another question. It stuns me that he doesn't want to learn this. He doesn't *want* to get sucked into a problem and let it mess with him for hours. How can he miss the magic of it? I want to show him.

Tate puts his head in his hands and sighs. He looks up at me with this spectacular mess of hair waving in every direction.

"This is the best part." I move my chair around to his side of the table and try to stay composed as I inhale the scent of him. Like coffee and a fresh shower and something sweet —is it the Sour Patch Kids?

My arm almost touches his shoulder.

Think, Aden. Math, math, math.

He's not as far from the solution as I thought.

"So, see this angle?" I draw him a diagram, and as I move the pencil, my elbow brushes his forearm. He makes no attempt to move, and our arms are touching as I finish the diagram. My arm tingles and I shiver. I want to lean into him. And then my body just leans itself into him without my choosing. Again, he doesn't shift away, as though leaning and arms touching and electricity are all a normal part of solving math problems.

"Sometimes it helps to think in pictures first, and then work with the equation. At least with this problem." I cover the lean with something mathy. Again I amaze myself with the ability to say anything coherent to Tate, especially when our arms are touching and there's leaning, and the floor just opened up and sucked the rest of the world away, leaving us here, like this.

There's a fleck of gold in Tate's otherwise gray-blue left eye.

"I know," he says.

"What?"

"There's that brownish color in one of my eyes."

"I said that out loud."

"You did."

I wonder if my face just feels warm or if he can see that I'm blushing. Heat. My whole body feels hot. I didn't know one could blush with one's whole body. I didn't know *a lot* before I met Tate.

Tate nudges me with his elbow and I smile.

"My dad knows," he says. "I was careless with last week's quiz. I just threw it in my pack, and he saw the freaking huge red C-minus scrawled on the top."

"What'd he say?"

"He thinks it's some fluke. Like it's the teacher's fault or something. Heaven forbid any son of his isn't thriving in academia. He wants to conference with her. Not happening. I'm a senior, for Christ's sake. I'm not conferencing with my dad and my calc teacher."

I'm not sure what to say.

"That sucks." It's a start. "There's time to pull it up," I add.

"But you're so distracting," he says.

No air. Tate just sucked all the air out of my body with one small sentence.

"What? I mean, why? Am I distracting?" Stop talking.

That was about ten octaves higher than my usual voice. I'm completely inside out—I bet he can see that everything inside me is all sparkly and dancy and laugh-out-loud because of him. I bet he can see, and yet he's still here with me telling me about his life.

He sighs. "I don't know what it is. You're easy to talk to. And I like what you say."

I have no idea what, exactly, *I say*, but God, I want to keep saying it.

*I*t's a shock to walk in on Jon and Marissa making out. On Jon's bed. Two days before his date with Sabita.

"Oh God," I say. And though I'm embarrassed and almost revolted, I stand there, staring at the two of them.

Marissa pops her head up.

"Aden!"

She sounds as worried as I am dumbstruck.

I'm reliving the trauma of sophomore year. The back of my brain is reminding me that this isn't my business. That I'm acting like a jealous girlfriend.

Marissa rolls from underneath Jon and pushes him off her.

I suddenly realize that I don't want to be standing here right now. I don't want to think about my brother's hard-on for my best friend. *Crap.* I just thought of it.

"Math homework time," Marissa yells as I walk into my room. I almost slam the door but think twice because I hate fighting with Marissa. I'm her anchor, and she's mine. I leave it open a crack and breathe. Jeez. What is it with me and needing to think about sucking in air lately? I wonder if I'm dying. That's what people who die do, right? They stop breathing.

Marissa will come in here after having made out with my brother, and I'll try not to think about what the heck just happened to my perfect little world of separates. Separate brother. Separate best friend. When separates collide, things get messy. And I've had enough messy. Maybe I'm closing my eyes. Maybe I'm not seeing what's real. But I'll hang on to this illusion for as long as I can because the thought of letting go, of letting separates collide and explode—it's terrifying.

I was never less a fan of Jon than when he dated Marissa sophomore year. And I've always been a fan of Jon, even when he's a tool. But it was bound to happen. We were all so close in age. Jon and I grew up around each other's friends. Marissa went from little-girl pretty to teenage knockout in a matter of seconds. Her breasts arrived in the summer between eighth grade and freshman year. Her mom, Cassandra, bought her a push-up bra because that's what a mom should do when her daughter sprouts breasts, and the rest is history. Every guy wanted her, including my brother.

It was awful. I tried to be the secure sister who supported this, because that's what I do. I'm the foothold for my dad, Jon, Marissa, because if I weren't, they might all float away. But I lost both of my best friends in a minute, not to mention all the attention I wasn't getting whenever Marissa and I were in the same room together. And observing brother-best-friend make-out sessions, the hand holding, the cuddling, was gross. I became the third wheel when I was supposed to be the engine. The center of things. And them together? It meant I was more alone.

I took it out on Jon. Lashing out randomly, refusing to let him have the remote under any circumstances. He didn't notice. Worse was that I felt like a jerk all the time for hating their relationship so much, and neither Jon nor Marissa noticed I was suffering.

I thought I'd be happy when Marissa finally moved on from my brother. It was Zane Casey. A junior. Had to be the lead singer of a band. He was tatted up, sporting pierced eyebrows.

I caught Jon crying into his pillow that night. I went in and sat down on his bed. I didn't care if he was embarrassed. A boy shouldn't go through his first real breakup alone. He should have a mom to tell him everything's going to be okay. And second best, a sister.

"Do you think I should get some tattoos?" he'd said to me through puffy red eyes. He was serious.

"No. I think you should wait on it."

He buried his head back into his pillow and shuddered.

I put my hand on his head and petted him until he fell asleep. A little boy. Soft, small whimpers, snot. My little brother. It hadn't occurred to me that maybe he'd loved her.

I couldn't fault Marissa for breaking Jon's heart. She couldn't help herself. So young, so messed up, so much life to live. Jon knew she was a flight risk going into it.

"Just fun, I swear," Marissa says now, as she pushes the

door to my bedroom open. I'm trying so hard to take myself out of this because I know it's not about me. Even though deep down I want it to be about me, it's not about me. It's about Jon and Marissa.

"Mutually agreed upon, no strings," she says.

I think about Jon's shiny red broken eyes and how I stroked his hair as he fell asleep that night. The whimpers. I realize I'm angry with Marissa, and I wonder if Jon will recover this time. I wonder how kissing, bodies intertwined on beds, can be "no strings."

Marissa tosses a candy bar and a soda on my desk.

"Peace offering," she says.

I open the candy bar with force and tear it in half. I throw the other half on the bed and sit down with math.

"Good, I'm glad you're sharing," she says. "I'm starving."

"Way too much information right now."

DAD

*I*f there are five nonlinear stages of grief, my dad is caught in a hamster wheel of anger, depression, and surrender. I've heard the last stage called acceptance, but for Dad, and mostly for me, it's never been about acceptance but surrender. A surrender like drowning. Relax, inhale, and sink.

It's been ten years since my mom died, but some days it might as well have been yesterday. My dad hasn't "moved on." What do people mean when they say "move on"? As though any one of us can control time or pain or longing. A few years after Mom died, my dad put most of our pictures of her into the attic. It felt awful to have her image disappear, because I was just starting to forget what she looked like.

"Dad, what happened to all the pictures of Mom?" I'd said. I was ten.

"Attic."

"Why?" My eyes had filled with tears then, but I wouldn't let them spill because I already knew he couldn't take care of me in the way I needed. I'd learned that the hard way when she died and he held me limply, saying so little. What was the point? My dad didn't know how to exist in sadness. For him, sad was a thing to beat and destroy. His anger started showing itself a few months after her death.

"Because it's time for us to move on," he'd said. "It's been three years." And there it was — *move on* — an impossible, elusive command.

"But what if I forget what she looks like?"

"All you have to do is look in the mirror," he'd said. "You're the spitting image of her." He had placed a hand on the top of my head and patted as if a head pat would grant me respite from having a dead mom.

And it was strange: the more of her he took out of the house, the more it felt like she was ever-present — this giant, un-talked-about energy hovering everywhere. And I get it. The pain of having lost my mom is too much for my dad. And surrendering to it means succumbing to the rage. Seeing that rage, being the object of it, is scary, but I understand it because it's in me, too. The anger. The surrender. The cycle is irresistible. The anger addictive. Because the anger? It touches the sadness like a match to lighter fluid, setting everything on fire. Anger is radiant and uncontrollable — a beautiful release. But the pain of sadness? It's ice-cold and so, so lonely. I'd rather feel the heat than the piercing, freezing pain.

To cope with the sadness and anger and emptiness, I started playing guitar. Because she played. If she was going to hover around with her energy everywhere, I'd find a way to channel it. I couldn't play her old twelve-string because it felt like touching the guitar with my own hands would erase her.

So I stashed her guitar in the back of my closet and bought myself a hundred-dollar Fender. It's one of the least expensive guitars on the market — my dad had saved up for my mom's thousand-dollar twelve-string for six months.

After the first month or two of struggle, I found that playing the guitar and singing was freeing. Music became an actual place I could go where my mom's energy wasn't oppressive; singing and strumming my guitar was deliverance — from not talking about her, from the pressure to "move on." I didn't have to be controlled or restrained when I channeled my mom or myself or let both of us intermingle in the music. I could just let it happen. Let me happen. My dad didn't say much when I started playing. But sometimes I'd catch him lingering in the hall outside my room, listening.

Now I hear him in the basement, welding. My dad owns a hardware store. Welding is his art. He welds sculptures and mailboxes, fusing together metal that won't bend unless under fire. I stand in the doorway of his workroom where the flames from his blowtorch hiss as the metal sizzles beneath the blues and oranges.

He looks up from the flames and steps back. He pulls the HAZMAT-looking mask up from his face.

"Hey, Peanut." Ah. *Peanut*. Check. We're okay right now. He's okay, approachable.

"Hey, Dad."

"What's up?" The trick is to gauge his mood. Green light if he uses a pet name. Don't engage him if you get gruff, one-word answers.

"You hear about Jon's date?" Talking to him about Jon feels like safe ground.

"No," he says with interest. He sets the torch down and wipes his hands on the apron he wears.

"Her name is Sabita. A sophomore."

"Huh. Interesting. Tell me more, my dear." He says this with clasped hands and a mock accent.

I roll my eyes at his sense of humor, but smile in spite of myself. "In your dreams. That was your only morsel, Dad."

I love this dad. The one who's dorky. The one who laughs. He only comes around every so often. But when he does, it's gold. It's safe. The other side of Dad would never do anything to hurt us, at least not physically, but that dad is moody and unpredictable.

ME

I've never kissed anyone. Unless you count that time in first grade when Bill Ditsman dared me to kiss Mike Fredrickson. I don't. Count it. My lips, my face, my whole body is untouched. I'm a senior in high school.

I wonder if it's because I'm not pretty. Or if it's because I'm overweight. I've read blogs written by sizeable women embracing their bodies and the men who cherish their voluptuousness. I even have a few pictures of "plus-size" models taped to the inside of my choir binder. But the truth is, who would want me?

I'm on my way to math class, wet hair from my morning shower thrown into a mess on top of my head, flip-flops slapping my heels as I shift my backpack from right to left, left to right. It's too heavy, and the edge of my history book keeps jabbing my butt through the fabric of the pack.

I look up, and to the left of the door frame, pressed into a wall of lockers, is Tate with his hand above Maggie's head, his lips on hers. My breath slams hard into my diaphragm.

It's a punch. She's wearing a loose, high-cut top and leggings, and I can see her thin—her stomach—because her arms are reaching up to wrap around Tate's neck. My eyes water involuntarily at the sight of them together. Kissing.

MAGGIE

I am not a quote person. *Don't lose hope. When the sun goes down the stars come out.* This is the quote taped to the front of Maggie Tiley's choir binder. It's accompanied by a picture of the sun setting behind a lake. Maggie has recently taken to sitting in front of me on the choir bleachers. I can smell the faint hint of her vanilla body spray. It makes me think of cupcakes.

I say fuck the stars. The stars don't provide vitamin D. The stars aren't a natural mood enhancer. You can't feel the stars. The stars don't even really exist anymore. They're just burnt-out memories.

Maggie turns around to look at me, and her hair flips a little, wafting the vanilla my way. I wonder if Tate would want to kiss me if I smelled like a cupcake all the time.

"Hey, Aden," she says.

I can't remember the last time Maggie and I greeted each other.

"Hi," I say.

"Are you trying out for the solo?" she says.

"No."

"You should."

I wonder if she's saying that so she can beat me. We all know she's going to get it. For a minute I consider it. I know if I could just let go and sing, I might just take it. But the thought of standing in front of our whole choir for an audition is nerve-racking enough to make me vomit the ugliest notes ever sung. This isn't open mic night. This is the audition choir where everyone's better than you and everyone judges everyone. Even me; I judge. I know that Sandra isn't as good as Chelsie, because Chelsie sings on key and her voice is thick and deep. Maggie? Her voice is beautiful, a perfectly crafted vanilla cupcake.

"Nah," I say.

She smiles and turns back around.

TATE

They say you have to know the rules before you can break them. It isn't true. There are no rules. Because whatever this is with Tate, it can't be named or boxed in. So there can't be rules. Or games. Whatever this is . . . it needs room to breathe.

Tate drives because he said he needed his "stick-shift fix." And because when he looks at me with that spark and his gold fleck, the word *no* evaporates from my vocabulary. My whole being is *yes*.

First and third gears are awkward, and I laugh as the car jolts. He stalls once and says, "I'm not embarrassed." We laugh loudly, for a long time.

Finally, he puts the car into fourth gear as we speed onto a dirt road, headed away from town, the wind blowing our hair into tangled messes, mine more than his. We're blasting the Shins, because now it's what we do together, before we move on to something more contemporary. He's singing at the top of his lungs while I try to move pencil across notebook paper, the wind messing with everything. No melody right now. Just words. About scars and love and rivers and holding hands and exploding.

I look up from what I'm doing and Tate glances at me, holding me there for a beat. I lose the rhythm of my writing when I try to go back to it—the words all muddled with the Shins' lyrics and the gray-blue of Tate's eyes.

Tate pulls into a drive-thru without us having discussed getting something to eat. It's late. We both stayed after school for math help, and then we hung out in the music room with Paul and Alana. Tate played piano while Paul, Alana, and I did terrible renditions of Broadway shows, laughing and falling into each other until we couldn't sing anymore. While we sang, Tate's gaze stayed with me, his eyes aglow, as though my laughter and happiness brought him joy.

We order Mexican junk food and sodas. Tate takes a bite of his makeshift nachos before we pull out, and then tosses the remainder of his chip into my lap. I eat the chip.

I concentrate on eating my grossly amazing fast-food burrito because if I don't, I'll start thinking about how badly I want to kiss Tate. Another chip lands in my lap.

"Dude," I say.

"Dude," he responds.

"I don't need your cast-off chips."

"You absolutely do need them."

I roll my eyes.

Tate parks the car in the lot. Simultaneously, we move our seats back. He turns the car off, but leaves the key in the ignition so our music can still color everything.

We eat together in silence for a song before I ask, "So do you go to synagogue every week? Is it like going to church?"

He smiles. "Isn't your mom Jewish?"

"She." I pause. I'm not going there yet. Because if we're there, this early on, then maybe having a dead mother becomes what defines me to him. Maybe it makes me seem sad. And I'm not. Not most of the time.

"She's barely Jewish." I know it's not real, but talking about her as though she were still . . . alive—it's like coming up for air.

"I mean, she doesn't practice or whatever it's called." Even though discussing my mom is liberating, I'm afraid if I keep going Tate will see through me to the truth. I'm not ready. So I'll hold on to this, too. Tell myself I'm in control.

"So what about you? Do you go? To temple or synagogue or whatever?" I say.

"I do." He says this with soft eyes, as though he knows my questions aren't just a curiosity, but a longing.

"Hold on," Tate says. He turns the volume of the music way up, opens his door, and runs around to my side of the car. "Come on. Out." He says this as he reaches for my hand, tugging me out of my seat.

"What are we doing?"

"Follow me," Tate says. He pulls me by the hand to the farthest outdoor table at the fast-food place. We're the only two people out here. Tate lets go of my hand and climbs onto the table. He puts his food in his lap and faces the setting sun as it barely dips behind the mountains. He pats the table, an invitation to join him, and extends his hand. I take his hand in mine and sit.

We sit side by side, our arms touching, legs touching, dangling next to each other. Tate hasn't let go of my hand. He sets his food to the side and pulls our held hands into his lap. The intimacy of this gesture catches in my throat, and I'm so glad I don't have to say anything right now.

He points with his other hand to the expanse of mountains and the waves of orange and pink clouds hovering over them. The sky is a torrent of sunlight assaulting massive storm clouds.

"Who needs a synagogue, though," he says, "when we have that?"

He's right. It's not just beautiful. It's holy.

I lean my head on his shoulder. He leans his head back down onto mine.

"But you still go," I say.

"Yeah."

"Why?"

He shrugs, pulling his head off mine, and I follow his lead, though I could've kept my head resting near his for longer. We sit together, eating in silence under the pink clouds the sun left in its wake.

When we've finished eating, we make eye contact and grin at each other before he leans his forehead into mine, pressing hard. Then he brushes a strand of hair behind my ear.

What is this?

I can't speak. I'm afraid if I move my lips, they'll betray

me, so I sit next to Tate, holding on to everything I could say to him. Surely he can see how much I care about him. But if I say it out loud, it could ruin this thing. Whatever is happening here, it's alive, but it's thin, wispy like the head of a dandelion.

Tate crumples the wrapper from his food and tosses it into a nearby trashcan.

"Three points," he says as he heads back to the car.

And just like that, the moment is over, and I'm left wondering if it was real.

MARISSA

*M*arissa drags me to the mall over the week-
end. I hate the mall. Not because I hate clothes or fashion.
I like clothes themselves—the colors, the variety of style
options. I loathe putting clothes on my body. Bottoms never
fit, no matter the size or style.

Bubbie, Mom's mom, used to take my brother and me on
"shopping sprees" at the beginning of every school year. That
was before she moved to Scottsdale. Relocating was her way
of "moving on." I can wrap my head around why she might've
left now—needing to leave the place and even the people who
remind her of the daughter she lost. At the time, it was a
desertion. Just another adult I couldn't trust to stay, like my
mom. Maybe I don't yet forgive her, but the older I get, the
more I begin to understand my grandmother's grief.

Bubbie is wealthy, and she likes high-end department
stores. I hate high-end department stores. I get the feeling
my mom hated them, too. My dad always says she wasn't
very high-maintenance despite having Bubbie for a mother.

Department stores—they're so sterile, and the elevator music makes me want to crawl out of my skin. I don't do "shopping sprees" anymore. I used to, because I wanted to be with Bubbie. Spending time with her still makes me feel closer to my mom. Back then I'd convinced myself that to know Bubbie was to know my mom.

Each year, Bubbie would get excited about our "spree" weeks in advance. She'd make a reservation for lunch and plan on spending hours at the mall. What Bubbie didn't know was that I couldn't have cared less about spending her money. I just needed her there. *Being there* is not, nor was it ever, Bubbie's forte, and when I was a kid, it made Mom being gone worse. Bubbie lives in some kind of la-la land where they drink cocktails every evening at five and skip to big-band music. You're not invited unless you're tra-la, skinny, and of age.

My brother would come away from the sprees with hundreds of dollars' worth of new clothes for the school year. I would come away with less than Jon, and what I did buy looked like boy clothes. Every time I'd try on a pair of pants, Bubbie would say, *Don't you think those are a little snug, darling?* I'd go a size up, and the waist would gape open, and even then, there wasn't enough fabric to cover the butt and thigh region.

Bubbie was disgusted with my body. I felt ashamed and awkward standing in front of her, trying on clothes. It made me miss my mom.

My worst shopping trip was when I came away with three baggy, pastel-colored cashmere sweaters and four pairs of ill-fitting pants. Despite alterations, department stores cannot work with my butt-to-waist ratio.

Bubbie was always skinny. Not thin. Not fit. Skinny. She smoked like a chimney. *Only ladies' cigarettes*, she'd say. Somehow she made smoking look classy, leaving a perfect ring of lipstick around the end of her cigarette, blowing smoke out the car window.

She'd offer us dessert, but never, *ever* partook. *Oh, I gave that up years ago, my little love*, she'd say as I downed another scoop of ice cream.

Now we drive once a year to Scottsdale, and each time she offers a shopping spree, I decline. She acts disappointed, but I wonder how relieved she is. She doesn't have to worry about fitting pants around my thighs or ass. She doesn't have to ponder the shame it is that I'm not some perfectly packaged ideal of a "young lady."

***

Marissa and I are at a trendy store in the mall. There's nothing expensive in here. Marissa is in the underwear section. She likes wearing sexy bras and underwear. *Everyone should have a dirty little secret*, she says.

"Aden. It's time for you to retire a few pairs of granny panties."

"Ha! As though anything here will fit me."

"Don't be silly. Here, try this on," she says, shoving a lacy red bra and its matching panties into my arms.

"I don't try on."

"Fine." She looks at the size tag. "These will fit you, trust me."

I sigh in the most dramatic way I can. The underwear is nice. I'd rather have these poking out of my jeans than my yellow patterned cotton. I wonder if my mom would want me to wear these, or if she'd think they're too sexy. I wonder what kind of underwear she wore. It occurs to me that this is a weird thought.

And then I think of Tate. I'd want him to see me in the red lace, not the polka-dot cotton. Not ever. I stare down at the panty set. I can't decide if they're taunting or tempting me.

"What do you think?" Marissa says. She's holding a strapless teddy up to herself and looking in the mirror. It's pink, sheer, and lacy all over. No doubt this teddy will be seen.

"Wouldn't this look spicy peeking out under a white tank?"

"*Spicy* is one word for it."

"Shut it, prude."

I have a vision of Marissa leaning over Danson's desk. That's all this thing with Danson is, though—flirting, leaning.

But I like it. The pink teddy. I try to picture myself in it, but I can't see myself as sexy enough. It's not that I don't think about sex, what it would be like. It's just that all my boxes are checked except that one. Excels at being a student, daughter, sister, friend, singer-songwriter . . . lover?

"Do you have specific plans for this spicy little number?"

"What if I did?" She's still looking at herself in the mirror, puckering her lips.

"Don't pucker. You don't need it."

"Ade, we all need a little pucker from time to time."

I roll my eyes. But maybe I could use a little change. Because thinking I'm not *whatever* enough (sexy, pretty, thin) is draining.

I think I'll get the panty set.

DAD

I'm six years old.

The front door opens, and instead of greeting us in the living room, my parents go upstairs, my mom's slender body leaning into my dad. She gives us a half smile and an even weaker wave before disappearing. Bubbie has let us watch endless television and eat three pieces of candy each in our parents' absence.

When we hear the sound of my mom retching, Bubbie turns the volume on the movie so high that Jon puts his hands over his ears. He's five, dressed in nothing but a pair of underwear and a cape. Jon and I look from each other to Bubbie. She motions to the screen as if to say, *Don't look at me—watch.*

When Bubbie goes to the kitchen, I climb the stairs quietly, on all fours. But before I can see my mom, like I'd intended, I need to use the bathroom. I flip the lid of the toilet and discover remnants of my mother's vomit on the sides of the bowl. I pee on top of the residual mess and flush once.

I stand with my head inches away from the seat, willing the evidence of my mom's pain to disappear. The bile remains, and I flush again, but the plumbing still runs, and water fills the basin, refusing to go down again. I wait and flush again, but it's sticky and the water in the toilet isn't strong enough to erase this mess.

As I stand, staring into the pot, I hear my dad talking in their bedroom.

Can I get you anything?

No, I'm fine. I'll be fine.

My dad's voice is low, almost a whisper. *I wish I knew what you needed.*

Me too.

The door clicks shut as he leaves her in their bedroom, suffering.

In six-year-old defiance, I do not wash my hands, but stand in the doorway silently, watching my dad leave my mom, his head hanging heavily between his shoulders.

When I think he's gone downstairs, I place my hand on the door handle, and just as it's about to twist open, I hear my dad say, *Aden.*

I turn to find him standing at the top of the stairs. I wave innocently and move to open the door again, but my dad says, this time louder and firmer, *She needs to be left alone right now, Aden.*

But.

No buts. Step away from the door. Now.

Can I just go in and give her a hug?
No, Aden.

* * *

I'd hated him bitterly then for keeping me from my mother. I couldn't have articulated it at six, but I knew two things: one, my mom wouldn't have rejected my affection, even when she was sick, and two, as much as I hated my dad in that moment for keeping me from her, I couldn't scream like I wanted. By then we already had an understanding about keeping a quiet house when Mom was sick. So even at six, I'd known what to do, how to act in such a way that kept the truth at bay in favor of counterfeited peace.

At the time, I'd thought my dad was protecting my mom. From me. But now I wonder if he was protecting me. From her struggle.

SABITA

*S*abita is sitting on Jon's bed. Jon's in the bathroom, and she hasn't noticed me yet. Whoa, her hair. I can see her messing with her hair. It's a symphony of black waves. A thick silk rope framing huge brown eyes, her skin maple syrup. She might be the most beautiful girl I've ever seen. I try not to think about the fact that just two days ago, Marissa was on that bed, making out with Jon.

I clear my throat before pushing the door farther open. I'm curious about her; I want to meet her. I consider leading with *You must be Sabita*, but think better of it for Jon's sake.

I smile and step into the room.

"I'm Aden."

She smiles back. It's a kind smile with a hint of laughter behind it. She has a really nice angular chin, and does she pluck those brows? How does she get that arch?

"Sabita." She extends a hand.

Oh, a handshake.

Her grip is halfway between firm and floppy, and I'm

not sure what to make of her, other than the fact that I pale in comparison. She's like beauty incarnate. Sickening, really.

Jon returns from the bathroom, and I'm aware that I've stepped into a make-out session break. I try unsuccessfully not to imagine the two of them sucking face.

"Hey, Aden," Jon says.

I flash him a look that's supposed to say *man-whore*, but I doubt he notices.

"Hey," I say. "Where's Dad?"

"Don't know." He's hanging on the door, gently nudging it closed, edging me out.

"Nice to meet you, Sabita."

Jon shuts the door in my face.

I think he might be over Marissa. Just like that.

I hang my new panty set on the top knob of my dresser drawer and stare at it. I wonder if the bra will make my boobs look too big. I wonder what kind of bra and undies Sabita wears. It occurs to me again that I should probably stop contemplating everyone's underwear.

JON

*S*pring of last year.

My dad and I are camped out under our lacrosse-game tent. Gatorade at the ready. The score is 3–5; Bentley is in the lead, as is normally the case. The tent and Gatorade all sound like a big deal, but the tent is portable—it takes five minutes to set up and take down. Sometimes lacrosse moms and the occasional dad will join us. Dad started investing in Jon's success as a lacrosse player when he showed talent in middle school. I think it gave him a purpose. He bought Jon the best of the best gear, even hired a trainer for him during the off-season.

Jon scores twice, quietly congratulating himself with the pull of his fist into his body. The team cheers and fist bumps and keeps running and running. I wonder how many miles they run in a game. I love the way Jon hurls the ball into the net, celebrates momentarily, and then just keeps on with the knees high and the jumping and the shouting to his teammates. He won't glance at us the entire game, but the not-looking—it's purposeful because he's so keenly aware of our dad there.

After the game he strides toward the tent, exhausted, straight for the Gatorade. They provide the team water and sports drink in big jugs, but Jon loves blue Gatorade, and Dad buys it in bulk at Costco. In fact, the blue Gatorade has been a source of the world's end in the past when my dad has forgotten it. Not because Jon was disappointed, but because Dad was so bent on making everything perfect. Today he even brought an energy bar, and Jon nods his thanks when I toss it at him.

"You played hard today, son," Dad says. The other team made a second-half comeback, but Bentley took it by a point.

He's proud and reserved, and did we just catapult back to 1950? You played hard today, *son?*

"Yeah. Important game," Jon says, but I notice he's not making eye contact with Dad.

"Two more games until playoffs?" I ask. Last year, Bentley lost the division championship by a game. That was right around the time Dad had started talking about a sports scholarship. *You take the team to State a time or two, you might have a shot at a full ride,* he'd said.

Jon takes a swig of his bright blue drink, wipes his mouth, and says, "Yup."

"You'll win it this year," Dad says.

Jon shrugs and glances at me with a flash of worry.

TATE

The halls of Bentley are empty. When I'm alone, walking these hallways, I own this place.

I turn left down the music and choir hall where Tate asked me to meet him.

I follow the unmistakable sound of the piano—bluesy chords overlaid with an excess of high flats and choppy, powerful, syncopated rhythm. Tate's shoulders are square and his eyes closed while his hands move passionately over the keys. I'm sure he meant for me to see this.

He looks up with wide, fiery eyes.

"Beautiful," I say. And I wonder how he can fish for a compliment with a simple look.

He grins.

"What is it?"

"It's called 'No Regrets.'"

"You wrote it?"

"Working on it."

"Is it true?"

"What?" He turns on the piano bench, his hands resting together between his knees. He's all arms and legs, but so at ease in his own skin.

"No regrets."

"Yep."

"How *can* that be true?" I think about all the mistakes I've made in life. If I regret nothing, then have I really learned?

"How can it not be? Regrets are"—he searches for the word—"counterproductive."

"But wouldn't you say if you live life with no regrets, you're almost living without contemplation? Like, *an unexamined life isn't a life worth living*, and all that."

Tate smiles. "I didn't say unexamined. It's the self-loathing that comes with regret. It's pointless. Time keeps on tripping."

"We must stop."

"Stop what?" His grin is full of mischief.

"Stop speaking in clichés and quotes. It's nauseating."

Tate smiles again. "That's why I love you, Ade."

Love. I know he didn't mean it *like that*, but the way *love* and *Ade*, those two words, just flew out of Tate's mouth so effortlessly—it's like he just pulled a grenade that went off inside me.

"Why?"

"Because you're a thinker." He taps the top of my head with his pointer finger, teasing me.

I laugh.

"But seriously. You don't see things the way everyone else does. You don't act the way everyone else does. It's refreshing." He gets up from the bench and grabs his backpack. And so I trail after him.

No MOM, but DAD

I started my period when I was eleven years old. Humiliated, I had to tell my dad. I wasn't expecting it, and sanitary pads were not on my dad's grocery list. We hadn't prepared.

"Aren't you a little young?" my dad said. As though I'd chosen to start my period. *Oh, I'm too young? Okay, then. Forget it. I'll start again in a few years.*

"I think I'm in the average range," I said.

"Okay, do you want me to run out to the store, then? You know, to, um, get the stuff you need?"

I wanted him to hold me and get as far away from me as possible all at once. I wanted him tell me it was going to be okay. There was blood in the toilet. Though I'd known what it was, I was scared.

"Yeah."

I didn't want to go with him. I couldn't go with him because the toilet paper wasn't holding. I'd ruined my underwear, and my lower belly ached. I got a dishtowel and stuffed it into my pants and went upstairs. I'd never missed my mom so much. I lay on my bed crying, waiting for Dad to return with a pad.

He bought four varieties. Huge packages of them.

"I'm sorry," he said, apologizing for so much. "I think one of these should work?"

It was a question. It shouldn't have been a question. I was supposed to be a little girl. Where were the answers I needed from him?

"Don't cry," he said. "We'll get through it. You're a young woman now. Tonight we eat ice cream and chocolate. Women like that. Ice cream and chocolate when they have their periods."

That night he had Bubbie come over and watch Jon. She winked and asked if Dad had handled everything okay. Did I have what I needed? Yes, I was fine.

"You are the exact same age your mother was when she became a woman," Bubbie said.

"Really?"

"Yes."

I burst into tears because I was scared and embarrassed by this change in my body. I knew what to expect, but I didn't have a mom to prepare me and talk to me and calm me. Bubbie brushed my hair back with her fingers and pulled the thick mass into a ponytail.

"And she cried just like you are now."

"Why?"

"Well." Bubbie smiled. "Probably hormones. And maybe she was a little afraid."

"Of what?"

"Change."

At that, I cried harder.

Bubbie pulled me into a hug. "We're all a bit afraid of change, my dear."

"I'm just. Afraid of losing her more," I said.

Bubbie's eyes welled with tears. It was unusual for her to show emotion, even sadness over my mom. I can't remember seeing her cry when my mom died. All I remember is having lived in her arms for a few days, the way she'd brush my hair back from my face and neck, my head in her lap as I stared into space wondering what dying really meant.

"You can't lose her more than you already have. And as you grow up, even without knowing it, you become more and more like her."

"I do?"

"Yes. And you look just like her." She tugged on my ponytail. Everyone says that. But when I look in the mirror, I can't see her.

It was the closest Bubbie had ever come to complimenting my looks.

"She's in you. In everything you do. You don't have to remember every detail of her for that to be a fact."

My dad and I went out for ice cream that night. We didn't talk about it, so accustomed were we already to avoiding uncomfortable subjects. We both loaded our cups with candy and chocolate sauce and never spoke of periods again. But I understood the gesture. I understood what it meant for my dad and me to be eating ice cream together on the day I'd started my period. And I was grateful for it.

DAD

I pull my car into the driveway, making sure I park it in perfect alignment. My dad has his . . . quirks. How we park the car is one of them. Especially because he's dinged the Honda a few times. He blames it on Jon or me for being incompetent.

I'm tired. More tired than usual. Maybe I shouldn't have eaten that candy in health class—the worst, most uninformative class in the history of high school classes.

It's unusually gray, almost foggy, today. The sky is like one giant cloud. Not dense but wispy, smoky, like you could wave it away. I wish I could.

"I'm home!" I throw my keys on the table in the front hallway and make my way up the half set of stairs to the kitchen. It's dinnertime. I stayed after school for choir sectionals and a physics help session.

There isn't much in the fridge. I grab a block of sharp cheddar cheese and some bread, take out a frying pan and some butter, and start making a grilled cheese. I flip on the stove and startle as the flames burst into a uniform ringlet. I mindlessly butter my sandwich and throw it into the pan. The bread is sizzling and I'm reaching to turn the heat down when I hear "ADEN!"

It's my dad's voice thundering up the stairs from the basement. I curse, having burned my finger on the handle of the hot frying pan. Our pans are too old—the handle shouldn't burn.

My back is turned to the basement stairs as I run my finger under cold water sputtering out of the faucet. My dad must've turned the water off again. I hear him clattering toward the kitchen, and I try to concentrate on cooling my finger. I go back to the frying pan and grab a dishtowel to hold the handle, trying to ignore my dad's anger, hoping it will go away. My hands grip the handle forcibly. This is not the dad I love. This dad woke up in an ever-empty bed and touched sadness. But he pushed that sorrow down and now he'll spit it out as anger. I don't respond to him because he'll be here any second, and if I don't yell back, maybe he'll stop.

I flip the grilled cheese. It spits butter out of the pan. I turn down the heat.

"What the hell happened to the downstairs remote control?" He says it more calmly than I'd expected.

I search my brain for what I might've done with the remote. I have no idea. Was I the last one watching TV down there?

"Have you asked Jon?"

"I would if I knew where the fuck Jon was," he says. "Jesus, what is the matter with you people?"

He's not calm anymore, and the emphasis is on *matter*. By *you people*, I think he means Jon and me, but I can't be certain. It seems so loaded.

I suddenly feel a surge of uncontrollable anger. "This is total insanity!" I say, or scream. This happens sometimes— my dad storms into a room, and I can feel a response rise up from deep in my belly.

My dad slams a few cabinets before he leaves the kitchen. My heart is racing, but I find a way to breathe through the anger. The anger was fleeting, a momentary loss of control, a reaction. In through my nose, out through my mouth. Huffing a sigh, I return my body to some semblance of equilibrium. I've got this.

There's something scary in the way my dad booms around the house—his voice and the things he says. But he's all bark and only a little bite.

The front door swings open, and I can hear Jon lob his backpack up the stairs so that it lands between our rooms. He has no idea he's just walked into a storm. Jon and my dad meet on the stairway to the basement.

"Any idea what happened to the downstairs remote?" My dad's voice is three notches louder than necessary.

"I don't know, Dad." Jon's voice is low. He never matches Dad's anger.

"Well, everybody *stop* what they're doing and get downstairs and *start looking!*"

I turn off the stove and toss my half-done sandwich onto a plate.

Jon and I make eye contact, not sure if we're friends or foes for this fight. We could blame each other, but we've learned over the years blaming each other leads to nothing good. It's hard to understand how the remote control goes from being just a remote control to being our saving grace. But dear God, we will find the stupid thing. I hate the remote control. I hate feeling like this.

I sprint to the bottom of the stairs, skipping steps as I go, my stomach tight, seized in my throat. Jon follows. I check the surface of the cocktail bar, my mom's antique crystal glasses hanging from a rack on the ceiling above, dusty and untouched since before she died. I move on to the heavy end tables from the 1970s. Inside the cabinets of the end tables are stacked black contraptions, old versions of Xboxes and Play-Stations. Why has Jon saved this junk? I'm looking in, under, and around, on my hands and knees, desperate, not for the remote control, but to end this.

Jon meets me on hands and knees. As I move to stand, he grabs my wrist and gives me a firm look, meant to call me out on my hysteria. I nod my understanding—he's right, it's useless for all of us to lose it—and force myself to calm. He's protecting me, or both of us, from tossing gasoline into this already raging fire.

I flip every cushion and finally find the remote under the couch. I'm sure my dad looked there, but it's in a weird spot.

Jon and I collapse onto the floor. I'm clutching the

remote, and we're silent save for our breathing, deflating from the frantic search. One of us will tell Dad that the remote's been found. But it won't matter. Dad will be sulking somewhere, perhaps lying on his bed, hands crossed over his belly. I'm not sure if he does that because he's ashamed of his behavior, if he even knows how it feels to receive his temper. Or if he does it because he needs to calm down. Or if he does it because he's still righteously indignant. I hate approaching him in this state. It's almost worse than the wrath.

We mutually choose Jon to go and tell Dad we've found the remote. Jon's less likely to make him angrier. Maybe it's because he's a guy and Dad's a guy (guy club), but Jon has always forgiven Dad his temper. And more so, he rarely gets angry himself.

Jon comes back from the delivery looking wounded, carrying my grilled cheese. He can't get mad because Dad's rage breaks him inside, each episode chipping away little pieces of his strength. I tear the sandwich in two and hand half to him. He eats listlessly, eyes glazed as the television flashes from image to image. I watch my brother and wonder what he holds back from saying or doing. Like if my dad and I weren't crowding all the space where anger resides, what would we learn about Jon?

We sit side by side without talking, and eat. The fluorescent lights buzz and flicker. Jon grabs the remote and starts flipping channels.

* * *

Eventually, Jon falls asleep, and I leave him there. Carefully, I ascend the stairs. I can see my dad through the sliding glass doors, hands folded over his chest as he looks out over the gloaming, dim-lit grasses, a beer resting on the ground next to him.

I could be walking into a landmine.

Our house was built in 1978, and it's a split level with a basement. My dad bought this house before he met my mom. It's seen the death of two dogs and a mother since we moved in. My parents built the deck themselves. It spans the entire back of the house. We don't have neighbors behind us, just a quiet street, and beyond are the open plains. The porch is my dad's favorite spot to sit quietly with a beer. The older I get, the more I appreciate it, too. It's a good place to be.

My dad is in his favorite lawn chair, wearing his plain gray hoodie. He must wear it every day when the weather turns. Before I say anything, I gauge his mood again as I stand in the now open doorway. He takes a slow pull of his beer, and I interpret it as a good sign.

I inhale. I hate walking on these eggshells, but I can't shake the fact that I could set him off with one wrong move. Are we past the remote control episode? Or does it still linger, its ember ready to flare any minute?

"Aden," he says. He sounds relaxed and kind. I can feel the tension in my body start to release. As I'm making my way to the chair next to his, it begins to rain. Big, thick drops that threaten to turn into slush or snow.

"You know I'm really a seventeen-year-old trapped in a forty-seven-year-old's body, right?" he says.

"Yeah," I say. "Except when you're four or five."

He laughs. "Yeah, except then."

We're quiet together as the rain increases its cadence, beating onto the porch's overhang. My dad takes a swig of his beer before saying, "So Jon tells me you're hanging out with a new guy?"

I eye him. It's alarming that Jon and Dad have talked about this. Jon knows about Tate because we talk about everything. And we both talk to my dad about *some* of this stuff. But still, what has Jon told him?

"Dad." I say this in the most teenage way possible, and then I laugh out loud at myself. I pride myself on not being the typical asshole teenager to my dad. He's had enough to deal with in life.

He's waiting for me to speak. He's looking out over the plains with squinted eyes. I zip up my jacket and pull my hood tight beneath my chin. Though we're sheltered, the wind is blowing enough to get us a little wet. The plains are a rich brown today with gray clouds cutting off the usually expansive horizon.

"Yes," I say. "I'm hanging out with someone new. And he's a guy."

"Anything doin' there?"

"What do you mean?"

I know exactly what he means. Not that I want to talk about it. Yet.

"New boyfriend?"

"No," I say.

"But you wish he was."

"Dad."

What could he possibly know about this? And why is he assuming that it's me who likes Tate and not the other way around?

"What? It's a crime to talk about crushes?"

"Don't say *crush*. That sounds so cheesy."

It makes the whole thing with Tate feel stupid and worthless.

My dad looks sideways with an eyebrow raised at me.

"Do you think it's possible to be fat and pretty at the same time?" I say.

"What?"

"You heard me."

"Aden, you're not fat."

I sigh loudly. *You're not fat* means nothing to me. What do people even mean when they say it? Do they mean *you're not ugly? You're not morbidly obese? You're not unworthy?*

"Dad, you don't need to tell me what I want to hear, okay? I just want to know what you think. Man to man. Can a girl be pretty if she's also fat?"

He scratches his chin thoughtfully, contemplating the question. "I think so. Yes."

Not what I was expecting. The long pause, the thought that went into it. What if the answer is just plain no? I'm not buying it. My mom was skinny. I wonder if it mattered to her—being thin. Why don't guys have to worry about this so much?

"Aden, you're more than pretty," he says.

"What do you mean?"

"You're pretty, but what makes you beautiful is that you're you."

"Thanks, Dad."

"So you do like this mystery guy?"

"Yeah," I say.

"And?"

"He has a girlfriend."

"And?"

"She's a lot of things I'm not."

"You can't be like anyone else, Ade. And no one, believe me, is like you. You're one of a kind." He winks.

"Dad? Even though I'm not her . . . I can't believe I'm saying this out loud . . . sometimes I get the feeling that maybe he doesn't, but maybe he could . . ."

I think about the way Tate's held my hand. I think about the fire between us. It can't be something I've just imagined, can it?

"Spit it out, Ade."

"I don't know. Have feelings for me."

"Yeah," he says. "I'm sure he could."

It's hard to reconcile this dad with one who rages over remote controls, but I have to. If I didn't take refuge in the warm, safe side of my dad, I'd be on my own.

TATE

The screen on my phone lights up. Tate.

"Hello?" My voice is light and alive, giddy.

"What are you doing tonight?" he says.

"Tonight?"

"Yes. Right now. Oh, nothing? Okay. Pick me up in fifteen. I have a plan."

He hangs up.

I almost text him about how presumptuous he's being, but I have only fifteen minutes to make myself look presentable. I throw on a little makeup and some jewelry.

> ME: *Text me your address?*
> TATE: *You're making us late. 3250 East Grove.*
> ME: *You're pushing it.*
> TATE: :) *Hurry!*

"Where are we going?" I ask as Tate buckles his seat belt and turns up the music with a kind of ease, as though we've been friends for years instead of a few weeks.

"It's a surprise. Make a left."

We pull into the synagogue parking lot of Temple Emanuel at five after six.

"Wait, what? Tate. I . . ." Everything I want to say gets caught in my throat.

"Come on." He looks at me. "It'll be okay. Let's go."

I sigh because he's pushy in the best way possible, and the never-saying-no-to-him phenomenon is intoxicating. So I open my door and try to keep pace with Tate's hurried stride. I don't have time to think about the fact that we're at a synagogue. Or the fact that I haven't been inside one for years. Or the fact that Tate doesn't even know my mom is dead.

The place is familiar. I realize as I'm sitting next to Tate, studying the Hebrew symbols painted on the ceiling, the rabbi's voice filling the room, that this is the exact temple where I once sat with my mother. My brother and I came with Bubbie on a few of the high holidays before she moved away, but after that, my dad never took us and we never asked. Maybe because being here without her feels wrong somehow. Like coming with her made me Jewish, but when she died, that part of me died with her. I don't have time to think about that because Tate is leading me to a set of chairs in the back, holding my hand. I try to remember to breathe. Without crying or overthinking this. Or wondering why Tate would go out of his way to bring me here.

As I watch the rabbi give a sermon about the importance of friendship, I wonder if he is the same rabbi who stood over my mother's grave at her funeral.

I glance at Tate as he chants Hebrew prayers. His face is relaxed, serene even. It must be nice to feel connected like that.

After the service, Tate puts an electric hand on my shoulder, and says, "Ready for Oneg Shabbat?"

"Yes?"

He laughs.

"What is it?"

"The best part."

We move into a banquet room outside of the temple. On a big buffet table sit several beautiful, fragrant, golden loaves of challah and bottles of wine.

I breathe deeply.

"Smells amazing in here doesn't it?" Tate says.

"I swear I'm smelling cinnamon."

"Could be. The Hebrew school kids all pitch in to bake the challah on Friday afternoons. Sometimes they spice up a few loaves."

An older couple approach Tate, the woman placing a hand on Tate's arm.

"Who is this, Mr. Newman?" the lady says to Tate, smiling and winking at me.

"This is Aden. Aden, meet my pseudo-grandparents, Mr. and Mrs. Weinstein."

"Nice to meet you."

Mrs. Weinstein shakes my hand. "She's lovely, Tate."

"She is," Tate agrees.

I can't make eye contact with Tate because I like this too

much and I'm afraid he'll see it. I like that Mrs. Weinstein assumes I'm good enough for Tate. I like that Tate hasn't corrected her in some awkward way. I like feeling as though I could be Tate's girlfriend.

I wonder if he's ever brought Maggie to his synagogue.

Tate hands me a small glass of red wine. "Allowed. It's for religion."

We exchange grins. I feel so happy. And closer to Tate. Closer to my mom in this weird way.

"So what do you think your mom will say?"

"What?"

"Aren't you going to tell her that you came to Shabbos service with me?"

I look into Tate's eyes and think about telling him the truth.

But instead I say, "Yeah. I'll tell her. She'll probably think it's cool." Which isn't that far from the truth.

* * *

Tate and I ride back to his house in silence until I say what I've been thinking.

"I don't want this night to end."

Tate smiles in a way that makes the air warm up and come to life.

"I don't want it to end either."

I pull in front of his house and set the emergency brake. He stays in his seat, still buckled.

I laugh. "So you refuse to leave?"

"Yes. I want three more songs. Play me something."

He closes his eyes while I scroll through my phone for three perfect songs.

He raises his eyebrows without opening his eyes when the first song starts to play. A Dustin O'Halloran piano solo. It's vibrant, emotional. Tate moves his fingers as though playing along. I watch him the whole song. His face says everything. Every nuance of the piece, every change in note, every refrain; his beautiful, expressive face betrays just how deeply he understands this song.

His eyes stay closed when the second song replaces the first. A duet. Ella Fitzgerald and Louis Armstrong. Tate smiles when he hears their voices. He reaches for my hand. And finally there is the warmth of his touch on my skin. So much heat where our hands collide.

And then the last song. "A Case of You" by Joni Mitchell. I can't help myself. While Joni Mitchell pours her heart out, I sing along with her. This is a song I understand with every ounce of my soul. It's about getting drunk on loving someone. It's about being able to hold all of someone, even if you're sick on loving that person.

When the song ends the car is silent. Tate unbuckles his seat belt and leans over the middle console. He kisses my cheek. It's soft, barely a graze.

"I can't wait to hear you really sing," he says before getting out.

MOM

At midnight I find myself at my desk, browsing the Temple Emanuel website. My head is so full with thinking about Tate and my mom.

The synagogue has a big congregation, so they have two rabbis. And one of the two has been a rabbi at the synagogue for thirty years. Rabbi Morrey. He must have known my mom. I type and erase the email until about two a.m., when I finally settle on:

> Dear Rabbi Morrey,
>
> My name is Aden Matthews. My mom's name was Vivian Bauer. When I was a little girl, my mom took my brother and me to synagogue a few times with her. She died when I was in second grade. She grew up attending Temple Emanuel. I was wondering if you remember her and if you'd be willing to tell me what you remember?
>
> Thank you for your time.

Sincerely,

Aden Matthews

In less than twenty-four hours, I receive:

Dear Aden,

How wonderful to hear from you! I have often wondered what happened to Vivian's family. I had reached out to your father a few times after she passed, and never heard anything from him. But I understand that he was in a time of deep grieving, and we lost touch over the years. I knew your mother quite well. Why don't we meet for coffee, and I can tell you what I remember?

Warm regards,

Rabbi Morrey

***

I thought about having Tate here. But if I'd invited him, I would've had to explain that I've been pretending to have an alive mom. And maybe this is something I need to do alone.

Rabbi Morrey and I sit outside in what little shade we can find. The sun is shining, the slight wind perfectly cool as it rustles through the remaining leaves on the trees. Rabbi Morey has just enough gray hair on his head to attach the black yarmulke he wears with bobby pins. The wrinkles on his face accent his smile. I can see why he's a rabbi, someone who's supposed to be a spiritual guide, a leader, a confidant. I feel like I can be myself with him. He's at once calm and warm, but still vibrant.

"You look like her," he says, and I wonder if it's just something you say to a girl with a dead mom. But he stares at my face without reserve for a beat, and I can't doubt his sincerity.

"So you said you knew her well?"

"She was a student in my Hebrew school. I saw her daily for a few years in a row. And after that, she came to synagogue services a few times per month. Until she got sick."

"What was she like? I mean, of course I remember her, and I know the stories my dad and grandma tell. But what do you think she was like?"

The rabbi inhales and smiles. He takes his time before responding. "I think she had the same light you do. But she didn't let it out at first. It wasn't until she grew up that she really let herself reach her potential. I knew her best as a middle schooler, just before her bat mitzvah. She wasn't always comfortable in her own skin. Who is at that age?" I wonder what kind of light and potential he's talking about, but before I have a chance to interrupt, he keeps talking.

"I believe she used to pal around with a girl named Rachel Labinowitz. You know, girls and best friends." I do. I think about Marissa. I don't know any friends of my mom's named Rachel. I wonder what happened.

I think he's going to stop there, but he takes a drink, then says, "Vivian was full of curiosity. I always knew she was destined to do great things."

I can't help myself when I say, "But she didn't, did she? She died too young."

Rabbi Morrey looks at me for a long while, and I look back, knowing full well that I'm challenging him to contradict me.

"Yes, she died too young. But she did great things. She lived. She was joyful. She wrote music."

"You know about that?"

"Everyone who knew your mom knew her music. It was one of her gifts to the world."

"But she never made anything of herself with it."

The rabbi chuckles under his breath. "No, she wasn't famous. Is that how you'd define success?"

I pause. I know he has a point. "Of course not. But"—I'm searching for the right words, searching for a way to defend myself—"wouldn't you say someone who pursues her dreams is successful? I'm not sure my mom ever did that."

"Ah. The pursuit of dreams." I like the guy, but I could reach out and slap Rabbi Morrey when he says *ah* like that. As though he knows anything about me.

"What do you imagine your mother's dreams were?"

The question halts me, because how could I ever know? And it's too late. How can I craft a mother for myself out of the faulty memories of others?

"If only I knew."

He nods his head, just once, as though he hasn't only heard what I've said, but he's felt it.

"You lost her early in life. It's hard to know things about her. Things like her hopes and dreams. Isn't it?" He speaks without pity; when he speaks, it's just fact. The urge to slap Rabbi Morrey evaporates.

"I did lose her early."

Silence sits between us, an easy, sad stillness. But despite my sadness, there is momentary peace in having shared a truth aloud.

The rabbi sips his coffee and then says, "She must've been in eighth grade when she sang a song she'd written at the Hebrew school talent show. It was the first time she'd ever performed. But I'll never forget how your mother surprised me that evening." He laughs. "I was nervous for her. Performing didn't strike me as something she'd be particularly good at. That was my lesson, though. Vivian was my reminder that people are never exactly as they seem, or as we perceive."

I close my eyes, trying to see my mom as an eighth grader, singing and playing the guitar.

"The lyrics had something to do with a bird taking flight. And I remember her voice sounded just like that. Free. She became the bird of which she sang in those few minutes. And she was no small bird. Your mother was flying with a six-foot wingspan."

The two pictures intermingle in my head. One is a hawk,

soaring over mountains, relishing the expanse of dusky sky. Another is my mother, singing and playing. And she's joyous in both pictures.

The tears come of their own accord, wetting my face and hands as I wipe them away. Without preamble, my tears turn into an unrestrained sob. I try to control it, but I can't. My body needs to weep. My soul needs to weep. And so I do, because I have no other choice. I'm not sure how much time passes. Five minutes? An hour?

Rabbi Morrey is not repulsed by this display of unrestrained feeling. Instead, he takes the napkin from under his coffee and hands it to me. Then he leans back in his chair and sips his coffee without staring at me or touching me. Without trying to make my reaction go away or become something else.

"I hope that's all true," I finally manage to say.

The rabbi leans into our table. "Of course it's true. I was there. I might be the only person in the room who saw her as she was—a flying bird. But see her I did."

I think about how the rabbi's story is just one in a collection of others' memories, small pieces of my mom stitched together in me. I may forever picture my mother as a hawk because I just can't remember how she looked as a person. But seeing her that way, as a bird soaring in the sky, feels like the closest truth I've known about her since she was here.

"Are all rabbis this . . . deep?"

He laughs. "Only the good ones."

When we part ways, I find myself wondering if I'll see Rabbi Morrey again. I don't know for sure, but it's comforting to know the door is open, a thin piece of thread connecting me to my mom.

MAGGIE, but really ME

I see thin girls everywhere. It's in the way they wear their jeans. What is it about autumn and a new pair of blue jeans? I just can't get my bottom into a pair. Or my thighs. The jeans are either too tight in the thighs — as in, I can't pull them up over my butt and thighs — or the waist gapes open at the back, revealing my butt crack. I'm in high school. It's just not practical to have plumber's ass each time I lean over to pick up my backpack or sit down in a chair. I can't think of a time in life when plumber's ass would be acceptable, except maybe if I was a dancer in a Jay Z video.

Maggie is wearing a pair of jeans today. They're slightly worn in the knee and faded in the butt and thigh. I know it's stupid, but I keep wondering, if I looked like her in a pair of jeans would Tate want me instead? But I'm sure she has substance. I don't think Tate is shallow enough to be with her just because he thinks she's beautiful.

Actually, I'm *not* sure she has substance. Not my kind of substance anyway. What do I even know about Maggie? She loves to sing. She's a soprano. Her breath, her pitch, vibrato, everything is perfect. If her cupcake perfume could sing, it would sound like Maggie. Silky, vanilla, thin Maggie.

I don't hate her. Not really. It's not her fault I'm like this and she's like that. I wish I could be like this *and* wear jeans. Without the gaping waist or bulging thighs.

Maggie smiles and winks at me as she passes back today's music.

I hate her.

JON

We sit side by side in the car, me and Jon. I'm driving. He's looking at the window, tracing designs into the fog. He seems mopey, which is unusual for him after lacrosse practice.

"You made the team, right?" I say.

"Yeah, of course I did."

"Bitchy. Jeez."

"Sorry," he says. "I made it, but the coach put me on midfield. I worked so hard last season proving that I'm an attacker. It just sucks. And the guys he put up front aren't that much better than me."

Jon has always been the athlete in the family. Not that I didn't try to keep up. When we were kids, I did all the same sports. The older we got, the more I noticed that he was better—he threw the ball farther, ran faster, jumped higher. And in middle school my body softened with the curves of womanhood, while he stayed thin with sinewy muscles. But I was never bad. The one sport I had on him was swimming. He didn't like the water in his ears, the chlorine in his eyes, the lick of cold water on his skin.

For me, being in the water, swimming, was worth the cold and whatever happened to my ears or eyes. It meant momentary weightlessness and muting the rest of the world. It meant feeling the water rush off my face as I turned my head to breathe. The forced rhythm of breathing and not breathing, of pushing my body forward when all it wanted to do was cave because my lungs were burning, my muscles aching. Swimming felt like answering a question my soul's always had.

I tried out for the swim team my freshman year. Everyone said it was easy to get on the team. Junior varsity was open to everyone. The swim coach was passionate about making swimming "accessible."

We had to wear the team suits for practice, and I hated the way mine rode up on my thighs. I had to shave in places I'd never shaved. The warm-up was five hundred meters of freestyle. I was the slowest on the team, and the coach kept calling me out. *Come on, Aden, what's the holdup?* The more he yelled at me, the tighter my bathing suit felt around my midsection, pinching my hips. I hated every minute of that tryout. It sucked the life out of the sacred experience for me that was swimming.

I never checked to see if my name was on the JV roster. I couldn't go back. And I was busy with schoolwork—I didn't have time to find another outlet for swimming. I quit.

Jon exhales loudly, as though it pains him to say, "Dad wanted me to play forward."

Oh, that. I forget about my jealousy and snap into mom mode because someone has to.

"Yeah," I say. "I get it. You worked so hard for an attacker spot. I wish you'd gotten it. But don't worry about Dad."

Jon's face contorts. "Yeah, right. Don't worry about Dad. Don't worry about the scholarship, right?"

I don't answer him. I'm looking seriously at Brandeis, a private school back East, so maybe I do need him to worry about the scholarship so Dad can afford tuition.

Jon leans back in his seat and folds his arms over his chest.

*I*t's Friday night, and Marissa and I are in my room, getting ready to watch an acoustic show at Ike's. It's not like open mic night, where anybody can play. The people who play acoustic shows get paid. It's a professional gig. One of these days I'm going to ask the owner to hire me. I just need to get up the nerve.

I love Ike's at night. The way it smells—espresso bean mixed with the must of books. I love the overstocked bookshelves and the eclectic art cluttering the walls. The way the dim light softens everything around the edges. We always see people we know there, but something about being at Ike's at night tears down the social barriers. I have full-on conversations with kids I'd never even say hi to in the hall at school. Or maybe they wouldn't say hi to me. High school is such bullshit.

The radio is cranked a few notches louder than normal. We have makeup, magazines, and clothes strewn over the bed.

"Maybe you'd fit this shirt," she says holding up a green sequined tank top.

"Maybe it'd fit my left boob," I say, thinking I'd never wear sequins to Ike's.

"Shut up, Ade. Try it on."

"No, thanks."

I ignore the shirt and lean into my closet, hopeless. How can it be so full of clothes and I have nothing to wear? There's nothing in there that will make me skinnier, prettier, more desirable.

"Okay, but I'm saying it's stretchy," Marissa says.

"Thanks."

"I wore it yesterday with a cardigan. Lance seemed to like it."

"I imagine he did."

I'm thinking that's the end of the Mr. Danson (Lance) conversation when Marissa says, "Every time he touches me, I swear I feel an electric shock run through my whole body. That must be chemistry, right?"

"Could be. I mean, I'm sure it is."

I'm a little more nauseous, the feeling rising like bile in the back of my throat, every time we talk about Mr. Danson. I thought Marissa's feelings would pass. But the more she talks about him, the more real it seems.

"So you stayed after school yesterday?" I say.

"I did."

Her response is frighteningly definitive. I want to say more, that I'm worried, but I'm afraid that saying this truth will push Marissa away. And no part of me wants Marissa far away.

Now she's all closed-lipped, when she's the one who brought the whole Danson thing into the conversation.

"Working on your sexay?"

She laughs.

"Something like that," she says. "Do you think I should?"

"Do I think you should what?"

"Have sex with him?"

"As though that's a totally feasible option." Maybe Danson is flirting with Marissa. But flirting to sex feels like a leap. He's our teacher.

"Let's pretend it is," Marissa says without breaking eye contact.

"And you want my honest answer?"

"Minus the bitchy," she says. Minus the bitchy. She doesn't want the truth.

"It might be sexy. But then what?"

"I don't know. I really care about him, Ade. He sees me as more than just . . ." She pauses, finishing with "a hot girl."

There's the crux of it. This whole thing about being understood by an older man for Marissa. With Danson she's not invisible like she is to her dad and every other guy her mom has dated since. I know what it is to need to be seen. Even if it's by the wrong person. Because as much as I want to be with Tate, maybe he's the wrong one. If only because he has a girlfriend.

"You know he's married with a kid, right?"

"I do," she says.

"So you really want to be that person?"

She looks at me, big eyes, long, mascaraed lashes. I'm already flinching, waiting for her claws to come out. Instead she says, "I've been her since the day I was born." And in her tone there's a note of sad resignation.

My ringtone breaks the silence. It's a lewd hip-hop song, the radio version—because it's so not me, it's funny. I dive onto my bed and reach for the phone as Marissa holds it over her head.

"Lover boy," she says.

I wrestle the phone away from her and swipe the screen to answer.

"What are you doing?" Tate says.

"Getting ready."

"For what?" he says.

"A hot night at Ike's. Want to come?"

"I do. See you there."

"Forty-five minutes."

"I need a ride home."

"You got it," I say.

My beam is involuntary.

Marissa raises her eyebrows. "We're taking him home?"

"What, is ultrasonic hearing your new superpower? You better be cool tonight," I say.

She laughs. "Who me? I'd never blow your cover."

I know she doesn't mean anything by it, but the way she says *cover* makes me feel like some sixth-grader with a secret crush. This thing with Tate, though—it's not like that. I didn't decide it. It decided me.

I glance at myself in the full-length mirror, and for a minute I think I look pretty. There's that word. *Pretty*. My long hair waves down my back in several thick curls, and the blue tunic I finally chose cinches a little at the waist.

"You look beautiful," Marissa says, putting her arm around me.

With Marissa standing next to me in the frame of my mirror, I lose the feeling, because I don't look like her, and I have it in my head that to be pretty you have to look like Marissa—be thin like her, curvy in all the right places. Marissa's hair looks tousled—like she just came from a sexy photo shoot at the beach. Her body thinner than mine. Her lips fuller. I envy the way she looks like an airbrushed model.

"I'm sure Tate will think you look beautiful, too," she says. And she means it.

* * *

Marissa and I sit at Ike's together. Her untouched black coffee sits next to my half-gone mocha.

I see Tate first. The tight brown sweater he's wearing takes the blue out of his eyes—they're totally gray. His hair is still wet from a shower. My mind drifts briefly to an image of Tate in the shower, and then we're making out in the shower, and I have to pull it together.

Tate ruffles my hair when he gets to our table. I don't like it. It's brotherly, and there's not very much brotherly in my feelings for Tate.

"Tate," Marissa says. "We saved you a seat." She gestures to the chair next to me as though he's some kind of king.

He gives her a slight bow and turns his attention to me.

They've only met a few times, but there's already something easy and familiar between Tate and Marissa. I don't mind it, though. Maybe it's because I'm what they have in common.

Tate helps himself to a gulp of my mocha. The familiarity of the gesture and the way he leans into me lights me on fire. We make eye contact, and I wish my eyes weren't so brown.

"So you're coming to Aden's thing, right?" Marissa looks at Tate when she says this, but he's still looking at me. He leans harder and turns to Marissa as though it's a chore to break our staring contest.

"What thing?"

Marissa raises an eyebrow at me before she says, "Open mic night. Here."

"Oh. That thing. I made a promise." Tate elbows me.

"Ouch," I say, rubbing my arm.

Marissa winks at me. It feels condescending. Like there's something cute about my feelings for Tate. But this isn't a Cody thing. With Tate, it's real.

When the lights dim and this week's performer takes the makeshift stage, Tate scoots his chair closer to mine. He drapes his arm around my chair, his body leaning into me so I can smell his shower. Suddenly breathing feels all sticky, and I look at Tate. He smiles and points to the stage like *pay attention*. If I could, I'd wrap my arms around his neck and lean my head into his. I wonder if he knows what he's doing to me.

***

Marissa stands outside without a jacket in the fifty-five-degree weather smoking a cigarette. Tate and I are off to the side, Tate complaining loudly about Marissa's "disgusting habit." I don't mention that I indulge in a drag or two myself from time to time. I just can't seem to get addicted to cigarettes.

Tate grabs Marissa's cigarette and stomps it out.

"What the hell?"

"It's time for a drive," Tate says. "Get in the car, ladies. Aden's DJ. I'm driver."

Marissa flashes me a vicious look, and I lean into her, pushing her toward my car. "Just get in, okay?" I whisper. She looks at me like I'm lucky she loves me so much—nobody gets away with pulling a cigarette out of her mouth.

Marissa sighs audibly, but gets in the back seat.

"Key me," Tate says.

I toss the keys to Tate over the roof of my car. He catches them and we smile, his eyes sparkling, as he gets into the driver's seat. The smile stays on my face as I wait for Marissa to get in the back. Then I slide into the seat next to Tate, as though this is where I belong. I flip through my phone and find the Shins. The old-school Shins. Tate rolls down all the windows despite the chilly weather and Marissa's unseasonable tank top. He takes us out of town onto a dirt road. He can't figure out how to open the sunroof. I laugh and take over. Our hands meet and we make eye contact. He squeezes my hand. My face turns warm and soft.

"Kissing the Lipless" comes on, and I blast it as loud as my retro speakers can handle.

Tate and I are singing at the top of our lungs, hands out the windows. Marissa is in the back seat laughing at us. She's here, but she can't be a part of this. No one can.

The night's air is cold and alive, and it pushes with force against my skin.

ME

I'm in eighth grade. I've tried out for the eighth-grade musical. It's a big deal because it's performed on the high school stage, and it's two nights instead of one. Rumor has it I'm a contender for the lead role. The cast list goes up later, and I can hardly stand the excitement.

"I heard some of the girls talking about you after gym yesterday," Amy, a girl in my class, says.

"Why would they be talking about me?" I say.

"The school play, silly!"

"Oh, yeah."

"Do you want to know what they were saying?"

"Sure."

"Well, most of them thought you were going to get the lead because you're such a good singer."

"Cool," I say.

"But, well, are you sure you want to hear the bad part?"

"Yes."

"The others thought you can't play the lead since she has to dance and stuff. And she's, like, super-skinny in the movie."

The lump in my throat is a little piece of my soul beaten out of my body.

I get the supporting female lead. Suddenly I have stage fright. And the girls were right. The one who got the lead is thin, if not downright skinny, and a far better dancer than I. It's Maggie Tiley. I hate my body.

***

I can't sleep. The clock on my nightstand reads 2:21 a.m.

I get out of bed and look at myself in the full-length mirror. My hair is borderline absurd, cowlicks making sections kink in opposing directions.

I think of Maggie Tiley. I now think of her as a cupcake. I love cupcakes. I love vanilla cupcakes with vanilla frosting.

Maggie isn't totally shapeless. But her curves are barely there. She's thin, and there's no question that she's pretty.

I force myself to keep looking at my reflection, allowing myself to see the soft lines of my hips, the places where my thighs bulge and dimple. I get on my knees right in front of the mirror, my breasts tilted toward it so I can see down my bra. I back up and practice cat-crawling toward the mirror. It wouldn't be so bad to be on the receiving end of this. I'm hot. Nothing I see is bad. My hair falls around my face, my eyes big and round, revealing everything.

I fall asleep by the mirror, and when I wake up next to it, I find the morning light is not so forgiving.

JON

The next night, I'm still battling sleep. I pass Jon's room on the way to the bathroom—too much pop before bed.

Jon's desk lamp is on and he's staring at his computer, rubbing his eyes. The clock reads 1:45 a.m.

"What are you doing?" I say. He must have eight windows open, all cluttered with numbers and diagrams. Probably one of his games. He closes the screen and pulls his textbook closer.

"Taking a break from memorizing formulas. I have a stupid chem test tomorrow."

"Well, it's almost two o'clock in the morning. Don't you think it's time to call it?"

"No. Thanks, though, Mom."

It's always weird when he calls me that. You'd think it'd be forbidden territory, but he pulls it out when he's feeling like a bad-tempered tool. I guess it's a big sister thing. Or he just needs to try on the word *mom* for size. But I wince every time he says it.

"I just haven't had time to study with practice, and then

Dad has me lifting every other day with this program he found online. I'm barely pulling a B in this class."

"I know it's not the best, but so what if you get a C in one class? Or on one test?"

"You don't understand."

"Try me."

"This test is a quarter of our grade."

"That is a lot," I say.

"So it matters."

"Yeah." It does matter.

If I'm being honest, I want Jon to get a scholarship because I know Dad can't afford two out-of-state tuitions. It's possible I'll get some kind of merit scholarship, but we all know that a sports scholarship goes a lot farther than a couple thousand dollars that says *great job on all those A's.*

I look at Jon hunched over his desk, head in hand, eyes squinted as he tries to retain information in the middle of the night.

It's also true I wish Jon didn't feel so much pressure.

"Do you believe in heaven?" I ask as I watch Tate toil through the math problem I finished in class. I stare at Tate's yarmulke, wondering if my mom believed in heaven, or if it even matters. Sometimes, being with Tate makes yearning for my mom impossible to hold. I want to tell her about him. I want her to help me figure him out. And I wonder, if she were alive, would I actually be Jewish? My mom's death took pieces of me I'll never know. But at the same time, when I'm with Tate, pieces of myself I didn't know existed are illuminated.

We're sitting on the floor, me and Tate, backs against the wall in the math hallway after school. Just the two of us in the whole corridor, but Tate's shoulder is pressed into mine. I'll never get used to my bursting insides with Tate.

"I used to," he says. "It's complicated in Judaism."

"What do you mean?"

Tate sighs and angles so we can talk face-to-face.

"Well, there's no official stance on the afterlife. Most of us believe in some kind of afterlife, but we're not explicitly told about heaven, or hell for that matter. Most of us don't believe in hell. But do I believe in heaven?" He pauses, shifting his weight. The half inch he just moved away from me is a mile. "I guess I have to believe in something. This can't be it, you know? You live eighty-something years, if you're lucky. Maybe you do some good in your lifetime. Maybe you're a total schmuck. And then you die? There has to be more to it, don't you think?"

"I guess," I say. "But heaven implies God. And I have a hate-hate relationship with God, if she even exists."

I think about closing the half inch between us and then some, but instead I grab the zipper of my backpack and start messing with it.

Tate smiles and repeats, "She." Like I bemuse him.

"If there's a God, then our lives must be some kind of game, right?"

"Either that or an experiment," he says.

"Yeah." I laugh. "A pretty sick experiment."

"Pretty sick indeed."

He mimes raising a glass.

"So you're not sure about the afterlife. But clearly Judaism is important to you," I say, pointing to his yarmulke.

"It is," he says.

"So what does it mean to you?"

"I don't know—there was this night, in Israel." He pauses, searching for the right way to say what he's thinking. "We sang Hebrew songs by the campfire, fell asleep in our tents for a few hours."

"I thought you said you don't sing."

"I did that night. There were thirty of us on the trip, from all over the world. But it didn't matter where we'd all come from, we were connected by something that felt so big." He sighs and smiles at me.

"So that night, we got up at two thirty in the morning for a sunrise hike up Masada. We'd spent the week talking and interacting, meeting Jews our own age living in Israel. Trying to dissect what it means to be Jewish. What it means to have this heritage. But on this hike no one spoke for hours. We just shuffled forward, climbing a mountain in dark silence. As though we were one." Tate crosses his legs, but we're sitting close enough that his knee rests on mine.

"When we got to the top, the sun was just dawning. And, it's so hard to explain this, but I've never felt more connected to who I am than I did in that moment, watching the sun rise over the horizon. It's like I was connected to everyone around me, and my forefathers, and all the Jews who've suffered and fought just to be Jewish for generations."

He turns to look at me, and I feel like I'm looking right at his soul when he says, "I didn't choose it. It chose me."

"And God?" I say.

"That"—he pauses—"is God."

ME, TATE, MISSY

*M*arissa and I are in the basement, getting ready to binge on '90s romantic comedies and chocolate.

"He must know what he's doing, right?" Marissa is twirling a piece of hair with one hand and eating chocolate-covered raisins, one solitary raisin at a time, with her other hand. The hair twirling might be cliché except that it's borderline OCD with Marissa. Once she starts twirling, she can't stop. I'm already feeling ill because I've eaten a bowlful of the candy, and now we're about to talk about Danson, a subject that is at once cringeworthy and absorbing. I take a swig of my Dr Pepper to offset the raisins.

"What do you mean?"

"Well." She searches my face for . . . what? Approval?

"Keep talking." I say, because it's the only thing I can think.

"He's asked me to stay after school three days in a row. How much more can we talk about the same freaking essay?"

She smiles to herself, and it's in the euphoria of that smile that I realize how serious she is about this. I can't know how she hopes this will end, and I can only guess at what she's getting out of it—validation that she's worthy.

"I think he knows, Missy." Because it's true. Despite not wanting to believe that Danson would flirt with or hit on a student, let alone my best friend, I think he does know. It's in the way she talks about him. There are some social cues you just can't miss. And I've seen Marissa flirt; it's not subtle.

"Marissa." I want her to know that I'm here, that she can tell me anything and I won't push her away or reject her like her parents have done, but also I need to caution her, to let her know that this could end badly. "This thing with Danson. I wasn't sure what it was at first, but it's starting to get more serious."

"It is." She agrees with me thoughtlessly.

"And, I'm worried about it getting out of control."

"What do you mean?"

"I mean, have you thought this through? He's our teacher." I hear myself say the word *teacher* out loud and realize Danson is no longer a favorite of mine.

"Well. He's not your teacher. Anymore."

"That's not the point, Missy."

Suddenly serious, she says, "I know. And I know what I'm doing. I think I might love him, Ade. He's not even ten years older than us. It'll be okay."

"How can it be okay? He's married. With a kid."

"That part." She hesitates. "I can't help it."

I wonder what it is that she can't help. The fact that a

teacher, someone with more power than he probably knows, someone with looks and charisma and manly hands, is paying attention to her? Or can't she help that he's married with a kid? What *can* she help? And suddenly I feel the same sentiment. I can't help it. Whether he has a girlfriend or not, I'm in love with Tate.

When my phone rings, I picture Tate's name lighting up the screen and smile when it happens, momentarily forgetting the weight of Marissa and Danson and all the things neither of us can control.

"Hey."

When he talks to me, his voice gets that laughing quality, and I could swear he's as giddy talking to me as I am talking to him.

"Hey." I say it in the same sort of laughing way and turn my back to Marissa, who's rolling her eyes as she pops her third chocolate-covered raisin into her mouth.

"What are you doing?"

"Watching movies with Marissa. What are you doing?"

"Nothing. Can I come over? My mom's on her way to the grocery store. She said she'll drop me off."

I glance at Marissa and mouth the words, *Please, Tate?* I'm pointing at the phone.

She rolls her eyes again and says, "Whatever."

I don't worry about whether she thinks Tate is crashing our girl time. We get plenty of one-on-one time, Marissa and me.

"I hope he likes Colin Firth. Or at the very least Hugh Grant," she says. We're deciding between *Love Actually* and *Bridget Jones's Diary*.

I toss a raisin at her and then make her pick it up because I don't want it melting somewhere on the cushions. There's nothing like Dad's wrath over melted chocolate on furniture.

When I hear the doorbell, I fly up the stairs two by two because if I don't, my dad will be first to greet Tate, and I forgot to mention he was coming, and my dad can't be trusted.

I'm at the top of the stairs, and there's Dad and Tate shaking hands. My dad is acting so normal. So friendly. I was sure he'd do the whole *What are your intentions toward my daughter?* thing, but instead it's like he's inducting Tate into the guy club. And then there's Tate. So at ease when he just met my *father*. It's like they're old pals. This is weird.

"Hey, you hungry?" Dad says to Tate. "I just threw a couple of steaks on the grill."

"Yeah," Tate says. "Starving. Just suffered through one of my mom's meatless pies for dinner. I'd love a steak."

"Great. Coke or Dr Pepper?"

"A Dr Pepper would be awesome, thanks."

I'm still standing at the top of the stairs, and I don't know whether to be annoyed or delighted at the comfort level going on between my dad and Tate.

"You and Marissa hungry, Peanut?" There it is. *Peanut.* Tate raises an eyebrow. I mouth *shut up*. "I could do a couple kabobs."

"No, thanks. We're gonna toss a frozen pizza in the oven."

"Suit yourself," Dad says.

"I'll leave you guys to it, then," I say, pretending to head back downstairs.

Tate pulls me into a half hug and ruffles my hair, but gently.

He's forgiven.

"But seriously, I have to go back down to finish the movie with Marissa."

"What are you guys watching?"

"Chick flick. Colin Firth."

"You coulda warned me."

"What'd you think we were doing down there, watching James Bond or something?"

"A guy can hope."

"It'll be over in half an hour. Forty-five minutes, tops. Then we can hang out."

My dad rescues Tate. "Come flip the steaks with me. They'll be done any minute. You like 'em rare?"

"A little pink in the middle is great, but I can't handle red."

And they're off. My dad and Tate heading to the grill on the back porch, discussing the way they like their meat, drinking pop. As the door closes, I hear both of them break into laughter.

After Tate eats his steak on the back porch with my dad —this is so weird—he makes his way downstairs. He and Marissa end up tossing raisins at each other while I gripe about melting chocolate on the couch or carpets. I'd be annoyed with the flirting, but somehow Tate manages to pull me into it, and I'm sky-high on being in the same room with him at my house, surrounded by a mess of chocolate-covered raisins.

"Let's play truth or dare," Marissa says.

"We're not in middle school," Tate says. He glances at me, and I shrug.

"Don't be such a prude. What do you have to hide?" Marissa nudges me with her elbow as though Tate can't see. I could kill her.

"Fine," he says, flopping down on the couch. "I'll play truth, but no dare."

"Why?" she says.

"Because dares are stupid, and I'm not making out with either of you tonight."

I don't know what it is about the way he says that, but it's humiliating. I can feel myself going hot from embarrassment.

"Fine. You in, Ade?"

Everything in my body is screaming *no*. Though there's so much I want to know about Tate and his feelings, I want it to be given, not forced out of him like this. With Marissa. I glare at Marissa. Here's where I'm weak. The part where I don't say *no* because I doubt Tate will ever give me the pieces of himself he withholds. So I let Marissa play this game. Because maybe this game will answer the questions that burn in me about Tate and his feeling for me, or his feelings for Maggie.

"What? It'll be fun. Come on, Ade. What do you have to lose?"

A lot. I have a lot to lose because what's at stake here—what I feel for Tate, it's big. And if I get shredded by this, or if what could be ends tonight, it'll destroy me. But maybe that's what I need. A little destruction.

"I'll start," Marissa says. She tosses a coin, and the truth ends up on me.

"This is boring," she says. "I know everything about you."

"Nobody knows everything about me."

"Let's see," she says. "Would you rather die in a fire, or drown?"

"Definitely drown."

"Why?"

"Quicker." All you have to do is close your eyes, and wait for that moment when inhaling is inevitable. Or at least that's how I imagine it would be.

"My turn." I end up on Tate. I want to ask him so much that would make a fool out of me. But I can't. I won't. I tread water with "Have you ever been in love?"

"Of course," he says. "Haven't you?"

My insides are ripping out of my skin. But is what I feel for Tate love? Can I love him without knowing what it is for him to love me back?

"I'm not up," I say.

Tate gets Marissa. "How many guys have you slept with?"

My mouth drops open. Marissa doesn't flinch. She looks at Tate, those wide eyes, long lashes, unblinking.

"Eleven is my best guess." She pops a raisin into her

mouth as though she's bored, and then flips the coin. She gets Tate and smiles.

"If you could date anyone besides Maggie, who would it be?"

When the question registers a millisecond after it's out of Marissa's mouth, it's like she's kicked me hard in the stomach. I can't look at her. I can't look at him.

Tate's sigh is loud, strained even. "I don't know," he says. "I hate these games. Not answering. Next."

"Dude," Marissa says. "You signed the dotted line when you agreed to play the game, and sealed the envelope when you asked about my sexual conquests, so play." Her eyes are ice on him.

"Fine." He looks at me for an eternity before he finally says, "Liz Weedle."

Something inside me just cracked, and I'm trying so hard not to cry. Liz Weedle. Skinny Liz Weedle with her Converse sneakers.

I wanted it to be me so badly I could almost hear my name on his lips.

Tate's confession ends the game, and he gets up to leave. Something is different. When he says goodbye, the fire that usually burns between us has fizzled. There is no mischief or glint in his gray-blues. I can't be sure, but as he turns to leave, I think I hear him exhale in relief.

"I don't think he was telling the truth." Marissa's voice reflects my own sense of defeat as we lie on the couch head-to-head, staring up at the outdated popcorn ceiling.

"Why?"

In the texture of the ceiling I see ripples of water. I think of diving into a deep pool and staying under for as long as my lungs can stand, the water suspending me in weightless escape, momentary freedom from everything, even breathing.

"Why don't I think he was telling the truth?" Marissa says, "Or why would he lie?"

"Both."

"I don't think he was telling the truth, because no one can miss the way you two are in a room together. It's fucking annoying. You're lucky I love you so much. And I don't know why he'd lie. Probably for the same reason you haven't told him how you feel about him. Because it could change things. And he probably likes the way things are."

I laugh, sadly. "I'm sure he does. It's like he gets the best of all possible worlds. Maggie, me."

"Yeah."

"But I'm left feeling so empty."

Marissa rolls onto her stomach and looks at me, softness and understanding in her eyes. "Want me to braid your hair?"

"Sure."

I slink onto the floor and Marissa sits up. She starts a tight braid near my temple, making a crown out of pieces of my long brown hair, rendering me a queen when I feel like a beggar—wounded, needy, and low.

DAD

*D*ad, have you ever thought about dating again?"
I say as the two of us sit on the porch together, after the dust
has settled from the truth or dare incident, and Tate has moved
on as though everything is the same, his eyes full of light every
time he looks at me. Even though he's still with Maggie. Even
though he wants Liz Weedle before he wants me.

I can see my breath, and beyond my breath is the pinkish
hue of the clouds hovering over dead-looking plains.

"No." He says it like it's a simple matter of fact.

"Why not?"

"Because nobody could be your mom."

So that's it? When your wife dies, you just give up on
love altogether?

I trudge on, tired of stuffing the truth down into
unreachable caverns. Tired of muting myself. "Just because
nobody could be her doesn't mean you couldn't be happy with
someone else."

"It's not that simple."

"Enlighten me," I say.

He finishes the last of the beer in his bottle, while I watch, willing him to respond. But he ignores me in favor of the view. As if I'm not right in front of him asking a question.

Something in me snaps. Because I'm angry. Angry at Tate for not loving me enough. Angry at my dad for not trusting me enough.

"Why can't you just let her go?" My voice is loud, cracking as the question forms.

My dad looks back at me, his eyes piercing.

"Okay, Aden, you want to talk like an adult. Let's. She's gone. There's no holding on or letting go. We have no choice."

"I'm not—"

He cuts me off. "Enough!"

I reach for something to say as my dad and I sit side by side. But I've been silenced by his anger and the wall he's built around my mom, as though he owns all the grief there.

The quiet of our unfinished conversation stretches as we look out over the grassy land, the color of the night having changed with the setting sun and our words.

I leave him sitting there alone and go to my room to do homework.

I stare at a blank computer screen, the glow of the lamp a rich, warm orange. I can't get my fingers to type the words of this stupid history paper, so instead I pick up my guitar.

I strum first A, then E-minor, then D, filling the silence between me and my dad—because at least a song can say what he won't.

MARISSA

*W*hat is it about him?" Marissa says. She's leaning against the locker next to mine. A messenger bag hangs on her shoulder, hitting her near the purposeful rip in her jeans. I don't know how she can get away with carrying a messenger bag when I have to haul a hundred pounds' worth of textbooks, not to mention binders and notebooks. But that's Marissa. Slightly underprepared, but ever more cool for it.

"What do you mean?"

"Tate. What do you see in him?"

"Shhhhh. Jesus, Marissa. I don't know."

I think about Tate and Maggie. Tate and how he doesn't want me second, but Liz Weedle. My skirt is too short today. I shift my backpack and adjust the skirt as best I can, but I look down and my leggings are too tight, thighs bulging.

We're walking through the thinning hallways, headed to my car. It's our lunch hour. It's a little stupid to take the car somewhere, but we're both craving pizza, and the only reasonably good pizza in town is a ten-minute drive. We'll probably end up eating our slices in the car on the way back to catch seventh period.

"Is it his eyes? Is it because he's tall? Are you thinking he has the whole tall, dark, and handsome thing going on? Because, I've got news for you, he's got a ways to go before handsome. Cute, maybe. But handsome? Meh."

I roll my eyes. "It's more than his looks, okay? Although for the record, I think he's handsome."

I wish the Liz Weedle thing had knocked it out of me. Maybe it should've.

"You guys are kind of crazy together."

"What do you mean?"

I know exactly what she's talking about. The way Tate and I are together. Like two sparklers. I wonder if it's like that with him and Maggie.

"You know what I'm talking about."

"I do," I say. "But let's pretend I don't."

Her turn for eye rolling. "It's like you're in some kind of secret club. It's weird and, honestly, a little uncomfortable hanging out with you guys. There. I said it. You definitely have something. Happy?"

I smile. I am happy. "I know. That's what it feels like when we're together. It's us. Him and me. And the rest of the world is just background noise."

"Thanks a lot," Marissa says. "But I think I know what you mean. It's like that with Lance sometimes, too. Just us. And nothing else matters."

A picture of Danson and Marissa flashes in my mind. I'm not sure she knows exactly what I'm talking about, but I guess she can relate in a primal-attraction sort of way.

"I just love being with him. I can't get enough," I say.

"Because of the secret-club phenomenon?"

"Yeah, that and because he sees me in this way no one else does. And I see him. It feels like I *really* see him, you know?"

I unlock the car doors, and we both get in.

"Like how?"

"I don't know. He just . . . gets me. We get each other, really. When we're together, it's like we step into this other dimension, and it's just the two of us floating through the world together. I guess that all sounds stupid."

"Hmph." Marissa pulls a cigarette from her backpack. She says she only smokes *in certain company, in certain circumstances*, but it's getting to be a habit. I start to say something when she cuts me off: "Don't worry. You know I won't smoke in your car. I just need to hold it. But yeah, I get what you're saying about Tate. It's weird. It sounds like—" She pauses, searching for the word. And then she says, "Love."

Is this what love is? To be fully seen and heard by another person and do the same in return? I think it could be. But then, he doesn't really want me. Not like that. I keep wondering why he's not attracted to me, but everything about the way he is with me says something different. I'm so confused, and all I really want is to be with him. I want to be his girlfriend.

"I wonder why he's with Maggie," Marissa says. She's holding her cigarette in one hand, a purple lighter in the other. She's flipping the lighter on and off, off and on.

"Because she's perfect." She can wear black skinny jeans, and shirts that show her midriff, and short shorts. I wear flowing skirts and tunics and long earrings.

"I guess. If you like that kind of thing. But you're more perfect."

I laugh. "I'm so far from it."

"Who wants perfect anyway? It's so boring."

"Well, at any rate, it's unfair to compare me to Maggie. We're nothing alike."

How I could I ever compete with Maggie? She's a vanilla cupcake; I'm a veggie kabob.

"That's good," Marissa says. "I was never a big fan."

I bet Marissa never gave Maggie Tiley a second thought until just now. But she's being the best friend every girl needs, and I love her for it.

MARISSA'S UN-MOM

I would rather suffer the loss of my mother, my frozen-forever loving mother-of-small-children, twice over than suffer Cassandra's mothering for a lifetime.

I was eight when I first met her. Marissa invited me over for a playdate at her house. We stayed in Marissa's room the whole time. We played dress-up. Marissa had a shoebox full of Cassandra's old makeup. It was the first time I'd been allowed to play with makeup without adult supervision. Not because my mom hadn't wanted me to, but because she was sick by the time I was old enough to do so. I poked my eye with a mascara wand that night. When we went to Cassandra for help, she yelled at Marissa, calling her an "irresponsible little slut." She was already drunk and slurring her words at that point. I was standing in the doorway to Marissa's room holding my watering eye. Marissa grabbed me by the hand and led me to the bathroom. We dabbed at it with washcloths and tried rinsing it. *Shhh*, Marissa kept saying. But all I wanted to do was cry out every time the abrasive washcloth came near my scratched eye.

When it was time for dinner, Marissa made us macaroni and cheese out of the box while Cassandra sat on the couch with friends, drinking and smoking. I knew deep down in my little-girl self that Cassandra wasn't really there to protect us. She was just there. I remember the smell of alcohol and cigarettes everywhere. Stronger in the living room but still present in Marissa's room. In her bed sheets. The faint smell of it on her clothes. Ashes. The color of Marissa's childhood is ash.

When we woke up the next morning, Cassandra had forgotten I'd slept over. *Who are you?* she croaked at me from underneath the hairy, big arm of the man with whom she'd shared the couch. I can't remember where Marissa was — she must've been in the bathroom. Cassandra's satin top swooped to the side, making one breast appear twice the size of the other as she lay pressed under the arm. *I'm Marissa's friend Aden,* I said. *Do you know how to make a bowl of Frosted Flakes?* she said. *If so, get me some.* Then she'd added *please,* as though it made up for having forgotten me. As though it made up for being the least protective mother on the planet. A mother who wore satin lace and slept under hairy arms and smelled of stale alcohol and cigarette ash while her daughter played with makeup and made boxed macaroni for dinner.

I never told my dad about the awful feeling of being unsafe at Marissa's — how must Marissa have felt her whole childhood? But I think he got the picture after a few playdates, because we rarely went to Marissa's house after that.

I have faulty memory for a mother, but Marissa? She's motherless.

*M*arissa and I lie on my bed while she flips through a magazine. I'm not a fan. Magazines just make me feel crappy about myself. Instead, I'm devouring a bowl of microwave popcorn. Marissa grabs a kernel every ten minutes and chews it agonizingly slowly.

"So truth or dare the other night?" she says.

"Whatdoyoumean?"

"You know exactly what I mean." She stares at me intently, willing me to talk.

"You're so melodramatic." I throw popcorn at her, and it lands in her mess of hair. Messy hair that even now is managing the bed-head sexy look.

"Watch it," she says. Then she adds, "You okay?"

I sigh. "He said Liz Weedle."

She sighs back. "I know. But I still don't think he meant it. He didn't even want to answer the question."

"Yeah, because he can probably guess how I feel about him and he didn't want to hurt my feelings. Let's just stop talking about it. I'm such a fool."

"You're not a fool, Ade. It was weird. The way he hesitated to answer. But can you imagine how things would've changed between you guys if he'd said you? It'd be weird."

"What would be so bad about change?"

Marissa doesn't answer but gazes at me as she pops another kernel.

I think about Tate's body leaning into mine or the way he held my hand the other day like it was no big deal when I could've spontaneously combusted in that moment and died happy. I don't want that to change.

Marissa looks toward the door. "Where's Jon?"

I roll my eyes. "Practice." I don't add that he's eating at Sabita's. I think Marissa knows he's been seeing someone, but she's never seen the way they look at each other.

"So what's the latest with Danson?" Part of me cringes at the question, but curiosity is burning my conscience, and it's a good way to change the subject.

"Lance?"

"Shut up."

She laughs. "Don't be such a freak, okay?"

"I will make no such promises."

"We . . . I don't know . . ."

"Good I-don't-know, or bad I-don't-know?"

Marissa makes a *hmph* noise, and there's something sad in that small sound. I look at her, and for a minute, I think maybe she is sad, like maybe she gets that this is a bad idea. Then she puts her head in her hand, sending her hair to one side, and says, "I stayed after class the other day. I wanted to ask about the flipping B I got on my last paper. He'd helped me so much with it. I thought for sure it was an A."

She says this like her grade is the point of the conversation. I know it's not, because Marissa barely gives a crap about her grades. She wants to graduate, but her aspirations beyond that are nil. I put my pencil down so she knows she has my full attention.

"I leaned. A lot."

"I'm sure you did."

"I saw him looking down my shirt," she says.

"Who wouldn't look? I'd totally look," I say. "I'm looking now." I have to joke about this or my conscience will explode. I'm left with the question of whom I can tell. If I tell another teacher or any other adult at school, not only will I ruin my friendship with Marissa, I'll get Danson in serious trouble. I know he deserves it. But something in me wants to protect him. I loved him as a teacher. He inspired me. In his class, I once wrote a piece about my mom and what it was like to lose her and then forget her. The comments Danson wrote in the margins of that paper were at once compassionate and insightful. He held my pain and pushed me further than I thought I could go. He made me rewrite the piece. I later turned it into a song. How can *that* Mr. Danson and the Lance of whom Marissa speaks coexist?

"Stop joking, Ade. I'm serious."

"I'm sorry," I say. "Go on."

"So, he's looking, and I'm talking about the paper, and

he says something, and before I know it, his hand is under my chin."

"I thought you were going to say boobs. Okay. Chin. Got it."

Marissa smacks my leg.

"What? Sorry. We went from boobs to chin. I'm with you." My conscience is screaming, a constant buzz in my head.

"Shut up, Ade. Seriously. Listen. So our faces are inches apart. I can feel his breath on my cheek. He has full control. And then our lips are almost touching, like he's going to kiss me. But instead he just brushes his lips against mine."

"He lip-brushed you?"

"He lip-brushed me."

We laugh.

"He tastes like almonds."

"Almonds?" I say.

"Yeah. Roasted almonds. Kind of sweet but mostly salty and totally addictive."

"Marissa," I say. "This is really dangerous." Though we've been joking, I say that last sentence with severity.

"I know."

"I'm not sure you do know."

She puts her hands on her hips, daring me to take this conversation further.

So I do. "What would happen if you slept together and someone found out?"

"There is no chance we'll be that careless."

The way she says *we* as though they're in this together tells me everything. She can't see him as predator.

"Someone could find out."

"They won't."

"Do you think you two will end up together?"

"I don't know, Aden. I'm not a child. I know this isn't happily ever after, okay? It is what it is."

"What exactly does that mean, Missy? *It is what it is.*"

"It just means I can't stop it. I don't want it to stop."

I understand wanting something forbidden, something you can't have.

DAD

I idle in the sliding glass doorway while my dad sits, hands crossed over his belly, eyes closed. The sky beyond our porch expanding over the plains never gets old. Tonight is cloudless. The sunset is a hushed coral glow. It's cold and breezy.

"In or out, Ade. You're letting all the cold air into the house." He sounds gruff, and I'm regretting my decision to approach. "Your brother home yet?"

I step outside and close the door, shoving my hands into my pockets. "No, said he was going to Sabita's after practice. I think her mom's dropping him off after dinner."

"Huh."

I can't tell what he's thinking.

He takes a pull of his beer and tilts it toward me. I take a swig, not because I particularly enjoy beer but because it's his peace offering.

When I sit down next to him, he puts his arm around me and I lean into his shoulder. The sun is down now, and we're left with a light blue fading to black.

ME

Bentley High is all jacked up about dances. There are three a year. Homecoming, the winter dance, and prom. I've been asked to a dance once. Senior Year Homecoming, last week. Chris Langon. I don't know anything about Chris or his family, but Chris has a long beard and long, greasy-looking hair, and he doesn't smell good. *Doesn't smell good* is an overstatement. He smells rank. But I talk to him every day after English because our teacher always lets us out two minutes early, and Chris's next class is in the same direction as mine. He's nice enough, but it's hard to be attracted to someone who seems against showering.

Chris himself did not ask me to homecoming. His *friend* asked me on behalf of Chris. In front of my whole choir section when we were hanging around before rehearsal. My choir friends laughed after the poor guy left the room. It was embarrassing. I said, *I don't know*, and then I had to say no the next day when the friend came back.

I bet Chris has a thing for me because I'm the only girl who acknowledges his existence. It doesn't make me feel good about myself. It makes me feel bad for Chris and shitty about everyone else.

My recent fantasy is that Tate asks me to the dance. Casually. It's not one of those ordeals where I waltz down the hallways with flowers or balloons. He asks me after school when we're alone.

When we go, I wear a long, slinky red dress that droops in the back. The dress is silk against my skin, and Tate runs his hand up and down my rib cage to my hips when we dance, his hand gliding on the dress, barely grazing my skin. He rests his chin on the top of my head while we dance, but we don't stay there for long.

In reality Tate will take Maggie to the dance, and I could never wear a slinky red dress.

TATE

$\mathcal{L}$isten," Tate says as I lean against the piano, waiting for him to pack his stuff.

Tate begins to move his fingers over the keys. His eyes are closed as he plays "No Regrets." It sounds different. He's slowed the rhythm, and there's something sadder about it.

"'No Regrets'?" I say.

"Yeah."

"It sounds like there might be a few regrets in there now."

Tate smiles without saying anything, and silently, we acknowledge the knowing between us.

I wonder what he regrets. There's something he's not saying, and I have this ominous feeling it has something to do with me.

"You drive," I say tossing him the keys to my car.

He smiles again and drapes an arm over my shoulder as we walk out of the room together, the echo of his song still lingering between us.

"*Drive* drive?" he says.

"Of course," I say.

I scan my phone for some good music and plug it in.

When I put on "Kissing the Lipless," Tate pushes his head back into the seat. He sticks one arm out the window, catching the wind, until the car revs with the need to upshift. So he shifts into fourth gear, cruising now on the open road, and then places his hand on the back of my neck. We're both singing, the wind blowing wildly around us, as though it's sucking anything that isn't right here and right now out of this car and away from us.

The song ends, trailing into something slower and sadder.

We take a deep breath at the same time. I'm thinking that moms and my mom have come up enough times in conversation, that it's time for me to tell him the truth. But I can't find the words.

He looks over and reads my mind. "Wanna talk about it?"

"I'm not sure."

"Why?"

He's pushing, and all I want is for him to hold this and me and fill me up the way he does. I know it can't last, but when I'm with Tate, the empty doesn't feel so lonely.

"It's heavy," I say.

"Try me."

"I lied to you about something."

"Okay," he says, taking his hand off my neck. Is he bracing himself?

"My mom isn't Jewish."

"What?" His eyes are wide, confused. Offended.

"I mean, she was Jewish."

"So she converted or something?"

"No." Here it comes. I wonder if he'll see me the same way. "She's dead."

"Wait, what? She died? When?" Tate pulls the car to the side of the unpopulated road and turns off the ignition.

"It was a long time ago."

"Why didn't you just tell me?"

"I guess I didn't want your—" I pause. "Pity. I didn't want you to pity me." The word feels like filth in my mouth, and I spit it out with the disgust I feel. Pity is what people feel when they're looking down on you from where they sit high.

Tate puts a hand on my knee, squeezing, and we sit in the beat of him knowing that I have a dead mother. We look at each other for a long time before he says, "I could never pity you, Aden."

I can feel the tears welling. The fear and then relief of his reaction threatening to bubble out of me.

I choke out the question: "Why?"

Tate exhales like he's been holding his breath.

"Because you are one of the strongest, most compassionate people I've ever met. And I'm so sorry that your mom died." He pauses again. "But you amaze me too much for me to ever think about pitying you."

Tate reaches for me, and I let his hand wrap mine in his warmth.

"So what happened?" he asks.

"She had ovarian cancer. I was seven."

Ovarian cancer. I've said something out loud I hate saying out loud. I just made her more dead. Ovarian cancer. The part of her that made her a mom killed her.

"Jeez," he says.

"Are you mad?" I'm crying now.

"No," he says. "I wish you'd felt like you could trust me with that."

"I just"—I breathe through a sob—"didn't want to ruin it."

"Ruin what?"

"Whatever this is," I say, finally acknowledging that there's something about the way Tate and I are that isn't normal.

He looks at me. "Nothing could ruin this."

I'm relieved that he knows, confused because it feels like he could love me. And I'm sad because talking about my dead mom makes me wish I had her.

It's silent and I'm more embarrassed. Drowning again. There's less air now than ever because Tate is here, and missing my mom is mixing with loving Tate and not having him. But this hole is a part of me. I can't pretend. I want him to love me.

Then he puts his hand on the back of my head and pulls me toward him. I'm stretched over the emergency brake and the stick shift. But somehow my head is buried in his chest and I've never felt more comfortable. I am held.

"I might get snot on your shirt."

He laughs and says, "I don't care."

He's stroking my hair, kissing the top of my head. My sad becomes his sad in this moment. This must be love.

"Tell me something about her."

He's soft and warm, and it's like we're holding this together, and maybe, just maybe, I can get a sip of air. I wish he would stay.

"I have her hair," I say.

"You got lucky. You have great hair."

I laugh through a blur of tears.

"I forget a lot of details about her. The older I get, the less I remember what's real or what I've been told."

Tate doesn't say anything else. He just holds me until I stop crying, and then we switch places and I drop him off at home. Even when I'm with him, I want more. I miss him when we're together. I want to cross the line more than I want anything. I wish he'd stay with me and love me, because I think he's the only one who knows how.

SABITA

I feel a hand on my shoulder and turn. It's Sabita. I can't look at her without noting how beautiful she is. Why does it matter so much? She smiles and gives my shoulder a small, familiar squeeze.

"Aden, hi."

I like her in spite of myself.

"Hey, Sabita. What's up?"

"Do you have third period off? I'm usually in the studio, but it's locked for some reason today. Want to hang out?"

Whoa. Sabita wants to hang out with me? Without Jon? Okay, this isn't weird.

"Okay, sure. I'm meeting someone at Ike's, want to walk over and join?"

I mentally kick myself for thinking it's okay to introduce Sabita to Tate. Even if she is Jon's girlfriend.

"Yeah, thanks."

"So what are you working on in the studio?"

"A marble sculpture. I think it's a turtle, but I don't know yet."

"You don't know yet?"

"Yeah." Sabita sighs. "I know it sounds all artsy, but I won't know until I get into it a little more. Like, whatever it is I'm creating has to present itself to me in a way. Well, that's how the art teacher describes it anyway. And I think that's true."

"I can understand that. It sounds a little like song writing. I don't always know what I'm writing about until I've written it."

"Yeah. Like that."

So we've bonded a little without Jon. Me and Sabita.

"You like working with marble best, then?"

"No," she says. "Marble is really new to me. And it's a bitch to chisel. Painstaking. I like clay the best, but the art teacher makes us choose something outside our preferred medium once a semester." She does air quotes around the word *medium*.

"Oh. I guess that makes sense. I mean, you are young. You never know what you might fall in love with once you try it."

I didn't mean for that to sound condescending. Did I?

"Yeah. It's definitely worth trying out all kinds of stuff." She doesn't seem to notice the comment about her being young. "I'm coming over for a cookout tonight."

This is starting to feel intrusive. She's invading my time with Tate and now she's coming for dinner? *And* she's proving herself to be a little awesome?

"You seem like such a great family, Aden. You, your dad, Jon. Thanks for being so cool with me."

I have no idea what she means about me being cool with her—I've barely talked to her. But just when I'm dwelling on her invasion, she makes some gracious comment and my walls are down again. She pulls her thick black hair out of her jacket and it falls around her face, onto her shoulders. I almost laugh because she's luminous. Absurdly luminous. I don't want to introduce her to Tate.

"Sure," I say. "I'm glad Jon's happy."

"You think?"

"I do."

"So who are you meeting at Ike's?"

"A friend. His name is Tate. He's cool. You'll like him."

"Friend?"

I must be see-through. "Yup."

"But edging toward more, right?"

"He has a girlfriend."

"Oh. Why isn't he hanging with her, then?"

Nailed it.

"We have a math arrangement."

Wow, that's not really it, is it? A math arrangement. We have a friendship.

"What does that mean?"

"I'm trying to help him pull his grade up. But we've become really good friends in the process."

"Oh. That makes sense."

Why do I feel like I'm selling myself short?

Tate is charming as ever. And I think he sees Sabita's radiance. How could he miss it? I watch him closely as we three sit together at Ike's. He gives nothing away.

Until he says, "I can't believe we haven't met, Sabita. I make it a point to know all the beautiful women at Bentley."

"Don't be a creeper." I elbow Tate.

What could be the most awkward moment in the history of moments with Tate is softened when Sabita says, "You're a lucky guy, Tate. Surrounded by beautiful women this morning."

"That I am," he says.

The pang of jealousy I feel toward Sabita is overridden when Tate drapes his arm casually around my shoulder as we make our way back to campus. Only, it's not walking back to campus for me, it's floating. I'm important. Even when I'm standing next to the most beautiful girl in all of creation, duly noted by Tate, I matter.

When we're all parting ways in the hallway, Sabita flashes me a look. I think it has something to do with the Aden-Tate secret-club phenomenon, but I can't be sure. She's aligning herself with me. She's good.

DAD/JON

I hear them downstairs in the kitchen. Dad's voice is raised and stern. Jon's voice is muffled, and he answers in clips.

I stop before turning the corner to the coffeemaker, where I'll add mocha-flavored creamer to the warmth of Dad's dark roast.

"Taking a break from the team is not an option," I hear Dad say.

"Just until I get my grades up, Dad. I can try out again next year when I have it more together."

"You'll miss your chance for a scholarship. No. That can't happen."

I can feel my insides tighten at the pressure on Jon.

"I can still get a scholarship, Dad."

"You'll stop spending so much time with Sabita if that's what it comes down to."

"No, Dad. Please. She's the only thing keeping me sane right now."

Jon's pleading. I'm still inches from the coffee. I wish I

had my hands wrapped around the warm mug as I listen to all this.

"Then what's your plan?"

They're silent, and I have to save Jon. I want to make this better.

But before I can offer to help Jon study or bend time so he has more hours in the day, he simply says, "I'll work harder."

It's not determination in his voice, it's sad resignation.

And Dad says, "Okay."

It's like he's missing the struggle Jon's laid bare. I wonder why he can't accept that Jon needs a break from lacrosse. It's as if when Jon said the words, they just . . . evaporated.

JON

The webpage for Brandeis University touts their mission: to transfer knowledge down through generations. I let the mouse hover over the homepage as I stare at the words, wondering what was lost when my mom died. Besides genetics and fading memories, what would she have imparted?

"What are you doing?" Jon leans over my desk, reading the contents of my computer screen. I shove him back.

"Knock it off, you snoop. I'm looking at Brandeis's website."

Jon plops onto my bed. "Oh."

"You ready for the motto?"

Jon grunts.

"Don't overdo your enthusiasm. It's *Truth, even unto its innermost parts*."

Jon repeats the motto in a mumble.

"What does that even mean?" he says, stretching out, his shoes now on top of my comforter.

"It means . . ." I walk to the bed, shove his feet to the side, and sit down next to him. "I think it's about perseverance

—learning a thing even when it's uncomfortable or inconvenient."

"The truth is almost always inconvenient." Jon studies me before he says, "Don't get too attached to Brandeis, okay?"

"Why?"

"Dad's always acting like this lacrosse scholarship is guaranteed, but it's not. Truthfully, it might be kind of a long shot."

"So?" The stupid truth. The *truth* is I do want him to get a full ride so there's enough money to pay for Brandeis.

"So who's going to send you to Brandeis if Dad can't afford it?"

I shrug. "I'll figure it out." Though, even as I say the words, I'm uncertain. "Besides, what will you do if you don't end up at some D-1 school?"

"I don't know."

I study my brother's creased brows as he stares down at his shoelaces, blue and coming untied. "You don't know?"

"No, okay?" His face and his defensiveness say he does know something he's not saying.

"What is it, Jon?" He's still not looking at me, and his untidy shoelaces have held his interest for far too long. Something is up. My brother has always been so busy doing what we all expect of him, playing lacrosse, keeping his temper, holding the silence. But maybe expectations weigh as heavily on him as they do on me. So I ask him, "What would you do if you could do anything?"

He sighs. "I've thought about . . . getting more into gaming."

"I'm pretty sure you can't *game* for a living."

"No, dumb ass. Like, computer programming. Designing games."

"Oh." My face must show my shock. "Really?" I knew he liked playing video games, but I had no idea it was a passion.

"Yeah, really. You don't, like, get the monopoly on doing what you want."

"I sure as shit don't, apparently." I cringe a little because I so often *don't* do or say what I want, but I think right now he's talking about Brandeis. "But you've never programmed before."

Jon rolls his eyes. "I program all the time, Ade. What do you think I'm doing in my room typing away at my computer?"

"Uh, homework."

"Uh, not exactly."

"So you're programming? Games and stuff?" He nods. "Whoa." I thought I knew everything about my brother. "Why wouldn't you tell me that before?"

"I just started over the summer. And I don't know. I don't have to tell you everything, okay? Jeez."

"Ouch." I thought we did tell each other everything. Or most things.

"Sorry," he says.

It's weird to think there are facets of Jon I don't know. "I'm here if you want to talk about it or anything."

"Talk about what?" My dad stands in the doorway.

I look at Jon, willing him to say it.

"Nothing," he says.

"Come on, Jon. Tell him."

Jon shakes his head. "Shut up, Ade."

"Why? It's awesome." Just the thought of Jon having dreams or ambitions beyond playing lacrosse and video games gives me hope. I think Dad should know.

"What's awesome?" Dad asks.

"Jon wants to be a video gamer." My brother glares at me. I shrug, mouthing, *What's the big deal?* He rolls his eyes.

"What's a gamer?" Dad looks from me to Jon.

"*Gamer's* not the right word, Aden. I want to design video games. It's *programmer.*"

"Well, whatever. He wants to do that."

"Fantastic," Dad says.

"It's not fantastic, Dad. I've been looking into programs, and I want to go to Rhode Island School of Design."

My dad stares blankly at Jon, as though he doesn't know his own son. Jon looks back at Dad and then adds, "They combine the technical side with design in a way no other school does. And they don't have sports."

"Oh," my dad says, his face falling. "Oh. Well, I'm sure plenty of D-1s have programming or design or whatever you need to be a . . . gamer, programmer, whatever." My dad stumbles over his words.

"Maybe," Jon says, "but D-1s won't have the design

component. Or if they do, it won't be as focused or ranked as high as RISD."

"Listen, Jon, I know you have a shot at a scholarship. Playing a sport you love. You're bummed you didn't get attacker this year. That's okay; you can still play the heck out of this sport. And get whatever degree you want. You can do both."

Jon shakes his head, sad and slow. Dad isn't hearing him. He can't see Jon outside of the box he's always fit in. And maybe I can't either. My brother's words ring in my head: *The truth is almost always inconvenient.*

DAD/MOM

*T*he spin of the ceiling fan is rhythmic as I sit hunched over my desk, working on a song. *Whoosh, whoosh-whoosh, Whoosh, whoosh-whoosh.*

Beauty is ~~love~~

What? Beauty is love? That's seriously the best I've got?

Put the pen down, Aden. You're ruining it.

I rest my head in my hands and resume listening to the whirl-whoosh of the ceiling fan. It sounds way better than my song at this point.

"Ade." *Whoosh, whoosh-whoosh.* "Ade, hello?" My dad stands in the doorway. He clears his throat.

"Hey, Dad. What's going on?"

He clears his throat again.

"Okay, now you're acting weird."

"What, why?" And then, in what sounds like a half-Russian, half-Japanese accent, which is not a reference to anything but his bizarreness, he says, "I'm not weird."

I laugh. "Right. Obviously."

"But I wanted to give you this," he says, handing me a piece of paper.

"What is it?"

"Just look at it."

I unfold the yellow lined paper and immediately recognize my mom's handwriting. I'd know it anywhere from all the old notebooks I have stashed in the closet. The paper holds a set of lyrics.

I look at the song my dad gave me and wonder where he got it. I thought I had everything. There is no title on the page.

"You should learn it," my dad says. "She was working on it when she . . . You know. I never got to hear how it turned out."

"Really? Do you have the chords somewhere? All I see are the words."

"Yeah, I know. She had some of the music figured out, but it must've been in her head. That's all I have."

"Where'd you find this, Dad? Maybe the music is there."

"I was just going through some old stuff. That's all there is. Promise. And now it's yours. If you want it."

"You were going through Mom's stuff?"

"Yeah."

"Why?"

"I don't know. It was after we talked the other night. You know, when you were asking about her."

"Oh." *That* conversation. I look up at him and notice the wrinkles between his eyebrows and around his mouth.

"So, you want these, right?" he says, and it's like someone's hit the pause button. He scrunches his eyebrows together, worried-looking. I wonder if it's hard to give her songs away.

"Of course I do. Thanks. What's it about?"

He grunts a wordless response.

"Again with the throat clearing, Dad?"

"I'm not sure what it's about, Ade. Could be me. Marriage, family. Who knows? It's yours now."

When you said
Love is everything
I believed you
I needed to
When you said
I need surrendering
I followed you
Into a place I didn't
Know
I'd never seen
Does that make me
A follower?
A believer?
Or just rash and blind.

When you said

Love is letting go
I let it all go
Again and again
With abandon
And now there's this
This little soul

She needs me
And I need you

I love her

And needing
And loving
It's all just one thing
Does that make
Me needy
Or loving
Or just poor and weak.

When you said
Love is everything
I believed you
I needed to
And now
I surrender
With abandon
Because

Needing and loving
Is all
There is left
Of me

I read the lyrics again and again, wondering what love
and surrender and weakness all have to do with each other.
Love is letting go and *I let it all go*. I think about the conversation I had with Rabbi Morrey about my mother's dreams,
and I wonder if she's talking about letting go of her dreams
in order to get married and have children. She was twenty-
four when she married my dad—twenty-five and twenty-six
when she had me and my brother. I'd never thought of her
as a young mom, but maybe twenty-five is young to become
a mother. She wrote that needing and loving are the same,
and the idea cuts me. I needed her like every child needs a
mother. And as I get older, the needing gets different, but it's
still there all the same. So missing my mom and needing her
coalesce in me until I can't tell which is which. But it doesn't
matter because sometimes, all I can do is surrender to the
pain of her absence and the pieces of me that will never be
fulfilled.

As I let the sadness of my mom's words seep into me,
the tune of her song seeps out of me. As though I've tapped
into something that has been waiting for me to discover it.
The chords are easy to pluck and strum. Without knowing
what this song meant to her, I know what this song means. To

love someone is a kind of desperate need. I feel it every time I think about Tate. But does loving someone, anyone, mean giving up a part of yourself?

ME

*T*onight is open mic night. It's one of many I'll play this year, but knowing Tate will be there, seeing this side of me, makes it matter more. I want him to watch me, to experience this side of my soul and fall in love. So I have to look beautiful, too. From my closet I choose a long flowing skirt and a formfitting shirt. I wear my feather earrings and dark eyeliner. I check the full-length mirror before leaving my room. I look good.

My dad is standing in the kitchen wearing his nicer clothes, khaki pants and a button-down shirt with a belt.

"Why the fancy clothes?"

"I'm going out," Dad says.

"Oh yeah?" I have a feeling I know where he's going.

"Yeah," he says. "It's a hot little place called Ike's. I know the band."

"I'm not a band, Dad. Just a one-woman show. Sit in the back, please." I'm smiling. I'm glad he's coming. He hasn't seen me play in a while.

Jon is in the kitchen drinking whole milk right out of the carton.

"You're gross," I say.

"Nah," he says, "this is gross." He takes another mouthful, then spits the milk back into the carton.

I whack him on the arm.

"Hey, that hurt," he says. "I was just kidding. The milk's almost gone. You think I'm a Neanderthal or something?"

"You think you're not?"

"So do you want me to wear some kind of disguise tonight?" Dad says, wandering into the kitchen.

"Can you?"

He laughs. "Only if it's these." He puts on a pair of fake teeth made to look like they're rotting out.

"Very country bumpkin," I say. "But I was hoping you'd wear the Dracula teeth and cape."

"Only if I get to paint fake blood dribbling down my chin," Dad says.

"But seriously, Dad, if you whip those teeth out in front of my friends, I will kill you silently while you sleep."

"I'll take my chances," he says.

* * *

I'm at Ike's, trying not to focus on droves of my Bentley classmates milling around before the show. I'm sitting at a table with Marissa and two guys. I don't know the boys, and they aren't interested in my existence. My dad, my brother, and Sabita are at a table toward the back of the room, and I wish I'd sat with them.

I'm staring above Marissa's head at a photograph of a woman lying on her back. She's in a grassy field. It's black-and-white, and the sun illuminates a few blades of grass and the woman's upturned cheek. The woman's hair is dark and long, extending beyond the reach of the camera's lens.

I turn back, feigning interest in Marissa and the boys' conversation about Instagram. Marissa stands up to refill her coffee. She's wearing hip-hugging jeans and a tight T-shirt. She looks great.

"So you're playing tonight?" one of the boys says.

"Yup."

I'm tuning my guitar, trying not to make eye contact.

"Are you any good?"

"Yup," I say.

I surprise myself with the answer. But it's true. I am good.

"Well, good luck," the boy says, smiling.

His kindness surprises me. I thought he didn't know I existed.

I scan the crowd for Tate. I wonder if he decided not to come.

The show starts. I'm slated for the third slot. There are five performers. I've forgotten all about Tate by the time the first guy is done playing. He has shoulder-length, wavy, honey-colored hair and a beautiful singing voice. It feels good to love someone else right now.

It's my turn, and I'm making my way to the stage, trying not to take someone out with my guitar. I sit on a small stool in front of the microphone and lean over the guitar, retuning a little, my hair reaching all the way to the strings, covering the sides of my face. I look up, but all I can see is the bright spotlight and a few strangers sitting close to the stage.

"Hi," I say into the microphone. I angle it down to my mouth. "My mom wrote this song. Her name was Vivian. She never titled it, but I call it 'Viv's Last Song.'"

And then I sing. I sing the beautifully sad lyrics my mom wrote. And I'm transported into the song. Each chord, each strum, each note, each word, it all means something as it comes out of me. As it comes *to* me — because that's what singing this feels like. It feels like letting go. Like floating helplessly down a river. I don't know what it sounds like, but I know what it feels like. It feels like I know this song better than I know my own heart. It feels like the only thing I should be doing right here in this moment is singing my mom's song.

The room is silent as the last chord melts away. I feel full and drained all at once. The applause is raucous, and the sound of it orients me as I make my way offstage.

I look for my dad. He's where I left him in the back of the room, his face buried in a cup of coffee. He catches my eye, sets his cup down, and raises his hands, miming applause.

He's smiling, but I see the sadness in his eyes. I blow him a kiss. I know he gets her song better than anyone else.

Jon is already surrounded by a group of friends. He looks at me and gives me a thumbs-up. His face is glowing. My brother's pride is the pillar I need right now.

I make my way through the crowd. A few people stop me to say *good job*. I smile and thank them.

I'm heading toward Tate. He stands at the back of the room, shadowed by a bookshelf. He hasn't broken eye contact since I spotted him. His gaze is steady and dark, but warmed by the upturned corners of his mouth. He is all I see.

I set my guitar on the ground and fold into his arms. He rests his chin on my head, and I'm so sure that he knows my soul.

DAD

When I get home that night, Dad is watching TV.

"Hi, Peanut."

I relax, knowing that tonight I get the dad I love. The one I need.

"Hey, Dad," I say.

I plop down on the other end of the couch.

Dad stares at the TV when he says, "I'm proud of you."

"Thanks," I respond, pretending what he's said is no big deal.

"You know, your mother . . ." My dad pauses because it pains him to say the word *mother* out loud to me. "She would've been proud of you. You are so much like her. She would sit on the back porch for hours with her guitar. Even at the end."

He stops, and I think that's all he'll say, because we so rarely talk about her.

"That damn guitar went to the hospital and back with her every time."

Then he sad-laughs. It's the kind of laugh that shouldn't

be a laugh at all. It should be a howl. But crying isn't something he does. Anyway, it wouldn't bring her back. So we laugh together, pushing the grief down into the depths of our bodies where it's more appropriate, where it won't betray us randomly. We laugh.

I think of my mom's twelve-string guitar sitting idly in my closet. Buried under old photo albums and clothes I grew out of in middle school.

The first song I ever learned how to play was Neil Diamond's "Shilo." My mom loved Neil Diamond. I remember one summer afternoon, my mom, me, and my brother in the car, each holding cups of soft-serve ice cream on our laps. The windows are rolled down, and we're singing "Shilo" along with the radio at the tops of our lungs, the three of us. The sky is swollen with afternoon thunderclouds, and it already smells a little like rain. My mom is driving with bare feet, one hand out the window, catching the wind. Her hair, my hair, it's a mess in the wind. We're not going anywhere in particular I can remember. Just driving, singing, inhaling ice cream and wind, being kids together.

TATE'S MOM

I want you to meet my mom."

Tate says this out of nowhere. He wants me to meet his mom?

"Why?"

He laughs. "Because I talk about you all the time, and she's curious. Plus you'd love her. She's kind of awesome."

Tate talks about me all the time? What does he say?

The word *mom* is stuck in my throat. Mom. Mom. Tate has a mom. Tate likes his mom.

"You think? That's a pretty cool thing to say about her —I mean, your mom." I sound like a frog.

"I wouldn't say it if it wasn't true."

"So when should I meet her?"

"In a few minutes. She's picking me up. I told her to come in."

"What?"

This is not something you just throw at a person. The meeting of moms.

"Don't freak out, Ade. It's not that big a deal."

Maybe it's not a big deal to him—he has a mom. Tate wants me to meet his awesome mom. Or her to meet me. I feel important and embarrassed all at once. I've met moms before, but it suddenly occurs to me that Tate has this great one and I'm not sure I know how to be, what to say to her. I wonder if I would've called my mom awesome if she were still alive.

He doesn't have to tell me. I know it's her as soon as she pushes the door open and walks through it. She wears a bright red scarf and large turquoise earrings. Even over the chatter of teenagers at Ike's, I can hear the faint click of her leather boots as she makes her way to our table. She's short, like me. We're sitting at the high tables today, and when she comes over, she's only a head or so taller than the table. A bold move, showing off his "awesome mom" here at Ike's. But that's Tate. He doesn't care what anyone thinks.

Her eyes are exact replicas of Tate's. In shape and the unusual gray-blue color. In expression. It's freaky.

"Aden." It's the first thing she says. And instead of extending a hand, she puts a hand on my shoulder and squeezes, smiling at Tate. "I've heard so much about you."

I like her.

"Well, I'm not sure what you've heard, but it isn't true. It's nice to meet you."

Tate smiles and folds his arms across his chest. He looks back and forth between his mom and me. Is he proud?

"I hate to say this, but you two are going to love each other. Aden, I might lose you to my mom."

"Most definitely," she says. "Now, Aden. Tell me every-thing. Has my son been treating you like the queen that you are?"

Now I know where Tate gets his charm. "He's been doing okay."

She nudges Tate's elbow.

"Ow!"

"I taught you better than just *okay*, son."

"Are you kidding? Aden is royalty as far as I'm con-cerned."

"Good. Tate tells me you're quite the academic? And a singer?"

"I'm not sure if I'm either of those things," I say. "But aspiring, yes. What do you do, Mrs. Newman?"

"Ah," she says. She pauses. "I do a lot." They have dif-ferent smiles, Tate and Mrs. Newman. Same smiling eyes, different smiling mouths. "But I get paid to teach college stu-dents."

"You're a professor?"

"So they tell me."

"What subject?"

"Art history, mostly."

"Really? Cool." That explains the scarf and earrings, the artful way she carries herself. "Are you helping Tate with Euro this year?" Tate's in a different section of AP European history than me. It's not art history, but we cover a lot about the art and how it reflects the political climate of the time.

"Come on, Aden. My mom's a professor," he says. "She makes me do everything on my own."

"Darling," she says, "you don't need my help. You have your own thoughts and ideas. But if you ever did need me for anything, history or otherwise, I'd help you find your thoughts." She winks at me like we're a team, against Tate together.

"See?" Tate says.

"I do see."

Would my mom have offered to help me with history if I'd needed it? I know the answer, of course. It's just that I'll never *really* know. Not like Tate does.

"So can I come to one of your shows sometime?" she says.

"You mean open mic night?"

"If that's where you sing. I've heard it's really something."

"Mom." It's the first hint of embarrassment I've heard from Tate. And I'm embarrassed, too, because Tate said my singing was something. To his mom. I look at Tate. He shrugs.

"You are good." The simple statement—the way it's fact for him—makes the butterflies in my stomach soar.

"Great," she says. "And maybe you'll come by the house sometime before your next show. Tate's been keeping you from us."

In this moment, I want nothing more than to "come by" Tate's house and be friends with his mom.

I hope she wishes I were Tate's girlfriend. I want her to walk away and say to Tate, *You need to dump Maggie for Aden.*

How can you miss it? She's perfect for you. And when his awesome mom says it just like that, it'll strike him. He'll stay up all night tossing and turning. *How could I have missed it,* he'll think. *Of course she's the one. I'm such an idiot.*

But I know this isn't a romantic comedy. And Tate's not missing anything.

JON

*I*t's the smell. A combination of BO, dirty socks, and sagebrush. I open the door to Jon's room without knocking.

"You're smoking weed by yourself now?" I say.

His bloodshot eyes are so predictable.

I notice the laptop on his desk, a small box open with groups of letters, numbers, and symbols, and another box with the outline of what looks like a robot. He's been programming.

"So what?"

"So it's a little pathetic."

I'm wafting the smell away with my hands.

He laughs. One roar too loud.

"You should try it," he says. "The bullshit in life, it feels so much more dull. But everything else, it makes it crisper. More beautiful." I look at Jon, wondering what it must feel like to melt all the pressure away with a few inhales. He lies down and holds the pipe out like I'm going to take it and toke right then and there.

"Hey, hey, hey," I say, kicking aside a pile of clothes to grab the pipe. "You'll spill it." I don't know why I care about him spilling the contents of his pipe onto his bed. I guess it's the carefulness Dad's drilled into me all these years.

The pipe is blown glass, a purple flower looping around the bowl. It's pretty, except for where the weed has burnt black crust on the inside of the bowl.

Jon closes his eyes, and I open the top drawer to his desk, placing the pipe and its contents there. Then I close his laptop screen. I contemplate the pipe and the remaining marijuana in the bowl. Jon is too far gone, and I don't like the idea of him getting high alone. I open a window and turn on his fan.

"At least get some air in here," I say. "Dad will be home in less than hour."

Jon's already asleep. He looks less like a little boy to me.

DAD

My hoodie is barely enough to keep me warm as I stand underneath the overhang of our deck. The wind is cutting, a knife edge in an otherwise temperate night. I tuck my hands into the sleeves of my hoodie and then into the front pocket. I'm too cold to sit, so I hover next to my dad.

His hands are bare, and I wonder how he can stand it.

"When did Jon start smoking pot?"

"What?" I say.

"Aden, don't play dumb. I live here, too. When did Jon start smoking weed?"

"I'm not sure," I say. "Maybe when you said he couldn't go to RISD."

"I didn't say he couldn't go. But he's a smart boy, Aden. He knows it'd be wasteful not to see where his lacrosse career goes."

"If you say so." I know I could say more, about Jon and what he wants, but I don't trust my dad to hear it.

"So?" I say instead. "Does he get grounded or something for the pot?"

I'm looking for Dad-the-parent to make an appearance in this conversation.

My dad exhales, long and slow. "No. He doesn't."

"I'm confused," I say.

"It won't do any good if I tell him not to do it. He'll just find some other way, some other place."

"Are you serious?" I say. It's not that I *want* Jon to get in trouble.

He nods his response.

"If it was me smoking pot, you'd be furious." My dad refuses to admit he has a double standard. Like how even though I'm a year older, he wouldn't let me ride a bicycle until Jon decided *he* was ready. He made me wait six months after I turned sixteen to get my driver's license; Jon was allowed to get his the day after his birthday.

"Don't be ridiculous, Aden."

"I'm not being ridiculous. What is it? Is it that I'm female and he's male?"

"Stop, Aden. You're two different people."

"Whatever."

When I huff inside, I think about leaving the door open a crack just to spite him, but I'm too afraid he'll rage about it.

TATE

Tate and I are cutting eighth period, the last class of the day, because for me it's health class, and for him it's gym. We shouldn't, but high school is strangling me today, and I'm always doing things I shouldn't with Tate, like loving him.

It's a beautiful day. Everything looks and feels like gold. The sun warms the yellow grass.

I love the sound of autumn wind rushing into perfect piles of raked leaves. I love feeling young. I love feeling this alive.

Tate drives us to a playground and parks the car. Without making eye contact, he unbuckles his seat belt and runs to the swing set. His arms are flailing as he gains speed down the grassy hill. He looks so free. A little stupid maybe. But free in it.

I have no choice but to follow.

We sit on the swings side by side, swinging as high as we can. My stomach flips—I don't remember that sensation from when I was a kid.

"Bet I can jump farther than you."

I laugh. "Well, you're a foot taller than me, so I'm sure you can."

"You're gonna let me win that easily?"

"Ever heard the expression *choose your battles*? I know which ones to choose."

He jumps, but I slow to a peaceful stop.

"Wuss."

"I own it," I say.

We sit together quietly, lazily hanging on our swings. Tate kicks the gravel beneath his feet. I try to breathe. I want this day to last forever.

"What's your worst fear?"

"I don't know," I say. "I think I've told you before."

"Tell me again," he says.

"I don't know. Like, living but not really living. Growing up and growing cold, numb." I pause. "That's the kind of fear you're talking about, right? Not spiders or snakes or something?"

"Definitely," he says. "And I get that. Sometimes even people in their twenties seem like they're just going through the motions. They're like robots."

"Yeah, I know." I wish I could find the right words. "I just, half the time I feel like I want to explode, you know? If I'm not passionate, fiery, what's the point?"

"I know what you mean," he says. "Do you think it'll fade as we get older?"

He reaches for my hand. His hand is almost twice the size of mine, and it's twice as warm. I don't answer him because I don't know.

TATE

I don't know how we ended up together at eleven thirty on a Saturday night other than that this is the second night in a row it's happened. My dad might kill me when I get home. He might not notice. But I can't care, because I'm consumed by all the space Tate takes up in me when we're in the same room.

"My parents are out of town," he says.

I almost choke on the Slurpee I'm sucking down, but instead I make a weird grunt noise.

"Where are they?" I'm trying to recover after the caveman noise Tate just heard come out of me.

"Some conference of the neurosurgeons in San Diego." He hasn't talked about his dad in a long time. I get the feeling his mom does all the real parenting and his dad is this looming, displeased authority.

"And they left you alone?"

"Yeah. It's only two nights."

We're quiet, and the atmosphere between us is a voltage so high I think I might spontaneously combust right here.

That would be a welcome relief because my insides are wound so tight it's all I can do to exist. Why is he telling me this?

"So do you want to come over for a minute?"

I just imploded.

"Sure."

* * *

"Let's go swimming," he says. "I want to see you in your element."

"What? You have a pool? It's midnight."

He smiles.

"I wouldn't exactly call it my element." I add. "I just love being in the water. Doesn't everyone?"

His grin stops time. "Nope. Some do, some don't. I'd say I'm neutral. Come on, Ade. Why'd you stop swimming?"

"Because . . ." Why did I stop swimming? Because I stopped loving my body? Because I couldn't be around my peers in a swimsuit? "I don't know why I stopped. Life just changed. I got busy."

"I don't buy it."

"Me neither."

He waits for me to elaborate, but I refuse to talk to Tate about being a girl and having a body. He chose Maggie—thin, cupcake Maggie—as a girlfriend. He couldn't possibly understand this.

"You can borrow one of my mom's suits if you don't think that's weird."

I want to get in the pool with Tate so badly, but he just said I can borrow his mom's suit. Which means if I do this, Tate will see everything. Every vein. Every dimple. Every roll. But I remind myself that it's dark, and I remember to breathe (that's a thing now because of Tate—breathing), and I say, hesitating, "Okay. I don't mind."

Before undressing, I stand in front of the mirror in my underwear. I'm wearing my new bra. It's sexy. My panties don't exactly match the bra. They're white cotton with multi-colored hearts all over. I think about coming out in the bra and panties anyway. They look okay. In the right light, I might look something close to desirable. I decide on the mom suit because I'm not sure which is worse—me in my underwear in front of Tate or me in his mom's suit.

The suit is of the old-lady variety, but it's two pieces at least. I can't imagine anything less sexy than Tate seeing me in his own mother's bathing suit, but here I stand in Tate's mother's blue floral tankini. I think of Tate and how free he seems. And in turn he makes me free. *Just be free*, I tell myself as I silently curse my reflection once in the mirror and head outside.

He's already in the pool when I come out sporting the glory of his mom's old-lady skirt tankini. All the lights in the house are on, and the aqua pool is lit from underneath. I can see every detail of Tate's body under the water. Which doesn't bode well for what he'll see of me.

He's not wearing his yarmulke. It's the first thing I notice about him.

He sees me staring and touches the top of his head where the yarmulke has left a crease in his hair.

"Naked?" I say.

"What?"

Oh. I just said *naked* out of nowhere to Tate. And he's in the pool.

"What? Oh. *No.* I mean. Without the yarmulke. Do you feel naked without it?"

"Oh. Yeah. A little."

I sit down and let my feet dangle in the water.

He dives under, and when he comes back up, he's right there—our bodies are almost touching; my leg is just brushing against his arm. He's always doing that. Coming into my space like it's no big deal.

"There," I say. I want to reach out and touch his hair, his face, and he's so close I easily could. I notice he has a little stubble around his jawline. "You got rid of the crease from the yarmulke."

He runs a hand through his hair. It should be my hand in his hair.

"Do you like me without it?"

"Yes. Do *you* like you without it?"

He smiles, and it's so warm, and his eyes say they love me because I just said something he *got*.

"I'm working on it," he says.

I guess I stumbled onto something with Tate and the yarmulke. All this time I've marveled at his bravery in wearing the yarmulke, but is it just a way to deflect? So people don't really see him?

"I'm surprised. I could've sworn you had more pride."

"We're all working on it, right? Self-love and all that?"

"So what's the yarmulke really about?"

Instead of answering me, he breaches all my personal boundaries, pushes his body into me, and I swear he's going to kiss me. Until his hands reach around my back and pull me into and under the water.

The water is ice crashing into my whole body. I stay under, letting the crash and the cold and the almost-kiss settle before coming up for air.

As soon as I'm up, Tate is splashing me. I dive back under. I forgot how much I love the water. Moving in water. Being underwater. Controlling my breathing. The way everything feels slower, smoother. I almost forget that I'm wearing a bathing suit in front of Tate, that my thighs and stomach and arms are bare and under a freaking spotlight.

I come back up and Tate leaps into me, grabbing me around the shoulders and waist, touching touching touching, and then he dunks me.

When I come back up for air, he says, "Was that too rough? Are you okay?"

"Yes, that was too rough!"

He comes closer—to see if I'm okay?—and I leap onto him. But he's so tall and sturdy there's no way I'm taking him down, so instead I'm just hanging on to him, my arms around his shoulders as he ducks underwater and flips me again.

He pulls me up this time, and somehow we're in each other's arms. Again, it feels like kissing him is next because that's what's supposed to happen when two people come together and make a bright-burning torch.

But Tate drops me.

He clears his throat before diving and swimming away.

In a split second I've experienced the elation of flying and the crush of crashing. Just like that.

He's across the pool, floating on his back.

This is humiliating. And nothing was even said.

I need to tell him I'm leaving, but I can't swim over there because I think he's built a force field between us, and if I cross it, I'll disappear before I get to him. That's what this feels like. It feels like crumbling. Like going from stone to sand.

I swim to the stairs and force my body to move out of the water. I hear Tate stand up behind me. I don't want to think about what Tate sees as he watches me exit the pool, skin and suit sopping wet, something like shame seeping from every orifice of me. All the places where my body has substance, fat. Rolls and dimples and no thigh gap. Maybe that's what this is about. Maggie doesn't have *substance*.

"You leaving?"

"Yeah. It's getting late. I'm not sure what my dad'll do if he notices I'm gone this late."

I amaze myself that I can talk without crying.

"Okay. See you tomorrow. Ike's?" he says.

Ike's.

"Yup." I say it like I feel totally normal. I'm not confused or crushed or wondering about everything that just went unsaid. I'm not decimated by his sudden coldness. I'm just the girl who'll share calculus and souls with him tomorrow.

"You're buying," I say.

ME

I stand in front of the mirror. I have on the only pair of jeans I own. I've resigned myself to wear the pair that show my butt crack from time to time. Because jeans companies don't understand what it is to have thighs and a butt, all in one body! As long as I don't bend down too much, I should be okay. I'm wearing a tight, teal-blue shirt. It dips in the chest, and I can't help but wonder if my boobs look too big. How did I let Marissa talk me into going to Seth Bernum's party? I can't stand Seth Bernum.

Seth and I have been in school together since kindergarten. We've been in the same classes countless times, and I could swear he doesn't remember my name. It's weird. And mean. I will admit he is incredibly handsome. Handsome is the only word for it. He has sandy brown hair with a spackling of freckles in the corners of his eyes. His lips are full and his jawline angular. And last year he grew. He looks like a miniature man. In a hot way. But he's a slimy, popular, douchebag, and if it weren't for Marissa, I'm not sure I'd even be allowed at his stupid party.

Marissa pulls me away from the mirror and shoves a Nalgene into my chest.

"I think the words you are looking for are *thank you*," she says.

I take a swig. "That is disgusting," I say, wiping the liquid from my chin. "Warn me next time. What the hell is that?"

"Vanilla vodka. It's low calorie and delicious."

"It needs a mixer."

"Vanilla is its mixer," she says.

I pass it to her.

"Can't drink until we get there. My brother said he'd pick us up."

Marissa's brother, Alex, is a real treat. He's twenty-one and works in a bar as a host and busser. His big aspiration —he'll tell you about it in full detail if you ask him—is to make bartender. He's one hundred percent nearsighted. It's like he doesn't expect to grow up and live life as an adult. I guess I can't blame the guy too much. He had Marissa's shit-for-parents. I don't get what makes him tick besides alcohol and random hookups. Maybe that's it.

My dad thinks I'm staying at Marissa's tonight. Technically I am staying at Marissa's . . . brother's. I told him Marissa's mom is out of town and Marissa needs someone to help her take care of the cats. He thinks we'll be ordering pizza, eating ice cream, and watching chick flicks. In fact, that sounds like a way better plan than Seth Bernum's.

I sigh and apply the last of my makeup. Eyeliner. Tonight it's thick because we're going to Seth Bernum's. My clothes are tighter than normal. This is all wrong except Tate said he might be there. I text him that Marissa and I are *in*.

I'm buzzing when we pull into Seth's neighborhood.

"Hey, save some of that for me, lush," Marissa says.

I laugh and hand her the bottle. She takes a swig because it's thirty seconds until we park.

Seth's house is the perfect replica of him. Obnoxiously handsome. It's surrounded by manicured everything — lawns, bushes, flowers. The driveway is brick, as is the walkway. I'm nowhere near manicured enough to be here. I want to burst out of my skin. I want to splash paint on the driveway, the house, the bushes, the color-coordinated flowers.

We can hear the boom of a subwoofer as we make our way to the door. It's a big mahogany door. Marissa walks right in. Almost into a woman who looks like the older female version of Seth. Her heels click on the marble floor as she comes to greet us. She's the human replica of the house. Everything manicured, trimmed, in its place. I'm wondering if the party's off and Seth is just downstairs hanging out with a few inner-circle friends when the woman sings out, "Keys in the basket, please."

She's holding a basket of car keys.

"No one drinks in this house and gets behind the wheel."

What? This party is sponsored by Seth's mom? Of course it is. Marissa pinches my elbow because she's as shocked to be standing here with Seth's mom as I am. She tosses the keys into the basket and smiles at Seth's mom.

"My brother is picking us up," she says. "Is it okay if we come back for the keys and car in the morning?"

"I'll set the basket outside the front door at seven," she says. "If kids don't have rides, they sleep it off downstairs."

The basement is as egregious as the house. There are kids everywhere. The basement is garden level, leading into the backyard where smokers are congregated under a canopy of white Christmas bulbs. Everyone looks a little better in the low lights of the basement, and *everyone* is holding a drink; there are a variety of bottles and bowls of punch-looking drinks strewn along the bar. I've never seen anything like this. No wonder Seth Bernum is Seth Bernum.

I'm assaulted by the remixed likes of Katy Perry blaring on the speakers. But I'm glad it's dark down here.

Marissa's hand is on my arm, and she's leading me to the keg. We have to wait because Jenny Sikes is doing a keg stand with three guys holding her legs higher than her head and a few other spectators are shouting, *"Drink, drink, drink."* I'm not drunk enough for this.

When Jenny is good and done, Marissa grabs two cups and says, "Chug." I do it gladly. And then another.

The edge is gone, and I'm talking to Justin Somebody, who's in my English class, while simultaneously waving at Alana and a few other choir friends. Fleetingly, I think about how it's strange I've never noticed English-class Justin until now. He's kind of cute. I look up from our conversation, and in a halo of blurry vision and strobe lights, I see Tate . . . and

Maggie. His hand is draped casually around her shoulders. Which are bare and brown and slightly freckled. She has a nice collarbone. I don't even know if I have a collarbone. I'm staring but can't be bothered to care.

Somehow I'm at the kegs again retrieving a drink for Maggie while she stands there with Tate. They're so at ease with each other, and I realize I've never actually seen them together outside school. I wonder if they love each other. And if they do, does it feel like being known?

When I'm back with the group, I grab the vanilla vodka from Marissa and hand it to Maggie. If I'm drunk, she damn well better be, too. It's insincere how buddy-buddy I'm being with Maggie, but everything feels so fuzzy and I'm in control. I think I am.

Marissa is tugging me away from Tate and Maggie while I'm babbling about how lucky they are to have each other and making a heart-shaped frame with my fingers. We're headed to the bathroom, but Marissa is pulled onto the couch by Josh Melling.

I'm in line for the bathroom behind Seth Bernum. It's just the two of us in the hallway. I'm too drunk to care about this being awkward.

"Nice party," I say. "The lights and all."

"Thanks, Aren," he says. He's falling-down drunk. I'm surprised he has a clue about my name.

Seth moves closer to me. He puts a finger on my shoulder and looks down to where my bra pokes out of my shirt. "I really like this shirt."

Finger is still there, resting on my person.

"Thanks," I say. I stumble into him as I say it, because his finger on my shoulder is throwing me completely off balance.

"Whoa there," he says.

Now he's touching me more, and I have to lean into him because him touching me is making me feel crazy drunk.

I'm briefly glad that I kept the sexy bra and panty set, and I can't breathe because Seth's fingers are trailing my collarbone. So I do have a collarbone. But everything is so hazy and wobbly.

We're stumbling into the bathroom together, laughing, and Seth says, "Wow, you have really big tits." He kisses me and plunges his face into my cleavage. I'm too drunk to care that he just said *tits*, though it registered somewhere in the back of my too-smart-for-Seth-Bernum brain. He's good-looking but a horrible, sloppy kisser.

Wait, that was my first kiss.

We're slobbering all over each other's faces, and Seth is clawing at my breasts. It feels like he's trying to turn the handle of a stubborn faucet.

I push Seth onto the toilet and straddle him so my breasts are in his face. His hands are around my back now, trying to unhook my sexy new bra. I don't like it, but I can't find the words to say so.

"Such great tits." He says *tits* again, and it's like the second sip of a scalding hot drink, a little less scalding, a little more stupid.

He can't figure out how to unhook my bra, and he's sliding clumsily off the toilet with me on top of him.

"Can we just lay down a minute?" he says. He means lie down. Can we just *lie* down. I inch off him, and he smiles up at me just before passing out on the floor of the bathroom.

And so I decide to pee. I look down at Seth Bernum as he snores on the bathroom floor. He's not handsome from up here.

Everything is fuzzy.

ME

'm on Alex's couch. I smell coffee, and pots and pans are clinking in the kitchen. Sound is magnified in my echoing head. Bacon. I smell bacon. I sit up and wonder how I got into Alex's ratty old T-shirt and sweatpants. Then I realize I don't want to think about how I got into Alex's clothing.

The sudden memory of Seth's hands all over my poor breasts makes me groan. I lie back down and pull the blanket over my face.

"That bad, huh?" Marissa says.

"Kill me," I say. "I smell. Horrible. Like a cow dipped in poop."

"You've smelled better."

She pushes an ashtray aside and sets a glass of orange juice on the coffee table. "Drink and go shower."

I do. Gladly.

"Seth Bernum?" she shouts as I walk into the bathroom. I slam the door.

I lean over the tub and turn on the faucet. I step into the shower. I can't seem to make the water hot enough, the pressure hard enough. I know I'm trying to wash away the shame and embarrassment. I imagine watching this feeling swirl into the drain with the soapsuds. I keep visualizing the shame disappearing. It helps a little until more of the night comes flooding back.

Tits. Slobber. Freckles. Lights. Sound. Maggie. Oh God, Tate and Maggie.

The shower isn't long enough, but I end it for the sake of Alex's water bill. I wipe the fog from the bathroom mirror. The eyeliner still lingers, but at least it's not dripping down my face. My eyes are bloodshot. I smell better.

When I emerge from the bathroom wearing Alex's sweats, Marissa sets a plate of eggs and potatoes on the table. And coffee. A steaming cup of coffee with milk and sugar. She smiles and slaps my ass when she passes, and I grab her arm and pull her into a hug.

"It'll be okay, hottie," she says.

"I know. Thank you."

"I still want details."

"Let me take my first bite of eggs."

"Only one. Then you talk."

After I finish telling Marissa about Tate and Maggie and Seth Bernum, she leans back on the couch like she's going to say something revelatory.

Then she says, "Whoa, Seth Bernum? You hate that guy."

EVERYONE ELSE and TATE

*I*t's Monday morning and I'm walking the halls of Bentley trying not to focus on the Seth Bernum Incident when I pass right by him, surrounded by a group of friends. All guys.

"Hey, Aden," he says. Seth hasn't said hello to me in the halls since . . . never. Seth has never talked to me in the hallway at school, and I liked it that way just fine. So him saying *hey* now? It's humiliating. The way he stretches out the word *heeey*. The way his friends snicker into their fists. Does he think I'm an idiot? I know he's making fun of me. I know what he told them.

"Hey," I say as quickly as I can eke out the word. More snickering.

"Party's moving to Ryan's next weekend," he calls as I turn the corner. I can barely make out the words *hope you'll be there again* and the sound of his boys laughing.

All I can hear is the word *tits tits tits* repeating in my head as I try to survive AP lit for the next forty-nine minutes. I look around and wonder if anyone's heard about the big hookup with Seth Bernum and how much he loved my breasts. *Tits.* Cows have tits. I am a cow. And Seth Bernum is a shithead.

Tate is waiting for me at Ike's after school. His giant latte sits steaming next to an untouched mocha on the table. He's reading a book for Euro. It's the first time I've ever wished Tate was Marissa. I'm not sure I need Tate right now, and I wonder why he's being so thoughtful with the mocha today. It does make sense, given the umpteen times he's forgotten his wallet and I've bought us coffees, Sour Patch Kids, and fast food with my babysitting money and allowance. What a mooch.

"What's with the cuteness?"

"Dunno. Thought you could use it," he says.

He arches an eyebrow, and I know he knows. I'm mortified. I should've known Tate is just enough on the outskirts of the inner circle to know about the Seth Bernum Incident.

I sigh and sit down. "Thanks," I say, covering my face with the cup and taking a long, slow sip. When I put the cup down, Tate is staring at me with those gray-blue eyes looking like I'm going to start spilling my guts right then and there.

Suddenly I realize that I'm angry. He doesn't get to know about this from me. It's not his. It's mine.

"Nothing to see here." I reach into my backpack for something to do.

"Okay." He goes back to reading his book, but he keeps glancing sideways at me. Any other day I'd love his attention, but today all I can think is *cow cow cow* when he looks at me.

"So, how far'd you go with him?"

Everything around us just burst into flames, and I can't hear anything because the ringing in my ears is so loud. So loud. *How far'd you go with him?* I think Tate just cracked open —a tiny sliver, but still, there's a cut where I can see something I haven't seen before.

Water. I need water.

Despite the chaos caused by Tate's question, I find the strength to get up.

"I'll be right back."

I think it's me talking, but the ringing, the flames in my body won't stop, so I can't know anything for sure.

When I get back to the table, Tate is looking at me like I owe him some kind of explanation.

"Just needed some water," I say.

"Seth Bernum? Really, Aden? The guy is a douche."

Again I can't focus because my emotions are rioting in my body. I'm electric because Tate cares about this. I'm furious because Tate thinks he gets to care about this. Like he owns anything about me. But doesn't he?

"Like you should have anything to say about it."

"What's that supposed to mean?"

"You heard me. Like. You. Should. Have. Anything. To say about it."

He shakes his head and turns back to his book. Now that

I'm on fire with the rest of the room, I might as well burn with it.

"What do you care anyway?" I want to make him say it. *Tell me you love me.*

"What do I care?" He looks at me like I'm supposed to know the answer to that question. He shakes his head. "You should know how I feel about you," he says.

I could almost laugh. I should know how Tate feels about me.

Right on cue, Maggie walks in with a gaggle of girls trailing behind her. I couldn't have staged it better if I'd tried. She sees us and waves like we're all just the best of friends. As though Tate and I weren't about to *go there*. As though I'm not still on fire and the rest of the room isn't burning to the ground because Tate cares that I hooked up with Seth Bernum and wants to know how far we went.

Mercifully, there's no big show of affection when Maggie and the two girls make their way to our table. *Our* table. I'm burning and broken.

"Did you have fun at the party?" She takes a sip of her hot drink, oblivious of the fire surrounding her, the flames between Tate and me. I wonder what she drinks. Hot cocoa? She sets the to-go mug on the table. Of course. It's a skim vanilla latte. "I was so drunk."

"Yeah, me too. It's all a little fuzzy." Then I add for good measure, "I'm not even sure what or who I did that night." I look right at Tate when I say it.

I think he winces, but it's hard to tell because Maggie is taking up so much space between us. I imagine her catching on fire but realize that's mean, sadistic even. I don't know who I am anymore. Someone who loves Tate. Someone consumed by Tate-love and the misery therein. This can't be healthy.

I grab a million pounds of books (why isn't anyone else carrying this much stuff?) and the mocha Tate bought me and get up from the table. I feel heavy and slow-motion as I push past Maggie and her friends and leave Tate there with them.

"See you in choir," I say.

I think I hear Maggie mumble, "What was that about?" as I press through the doors.

*S*o Jon and this sophomore girl are serious?"

"Yeah. Her name is Sabita."

Marissa's trying not to sound jealous, but she is. I don't know how she missed the Sabita and Jon thing developing. It's been almost two months. I guess Marissa has been hyper-focused on Danson; everything beyond him is foggy.

"A sophomore?"

This is an invitation to jump in with a nasty comment, but my loyalty to Jon holds steady.

"Yup."

I surprise myself with the instinct to defend Sabita. She's Jon's choice. I hold back the urge to say anything else. I don't want to say anything that might hurt Marissa either.

"She pretty?"

Pretty doesn't begin to describe her, Marissa. She's beautiful. And she has personality, spirit.

"Yeah. She's pretty." I show Marissa some mercy.

JON

*T*he whole house smells like weed again, and my dad is home this time. I wonder how he can stand knowing that Jon is upstairs with his girlfriend smoking pot and making out.

I hate that I have to pass Jon's open door on the way to my room. He and Sabita are sprawled on his bed, intermittently breaking into laughter.

"Aden," he says as I pass his door.

"Hey, Jonathan."

I'm trying to make it to my room without having to interact. All I can think about is Tate and how awful I feel about Seth and everyone knowing thanks to social media, which mercifully, I've refused to check in the last forty-eight hours.

"What's the word?"

"Just gonna do some homework. Which is what you should be doing."

Please stop talking to me, I think. *I just want to sulk in my room.*

"Thanks, *Mom*." He laughs, but it's not funny. Her absence is its own presence.

Sabita sits up onto her elbows. She looks like a goddess. *Cow cow cow.* My stupid brain won't stop taunting me. "Hey, Aden," she says.

"Hey, Sabita." And then I add, "Where'd you guys get the weed?"

"A girl I know," Jon says. "Want a toke?"

I sigh. Yes. I do. I wonder if the weed would make me feel like less of a fool. Or cow, as the case is. If I got crazy-high right now, would it feel better to know that Tate knows? Would it make me stop obsessing over the possibility that he cares because he *cares*?

But I'm not ready to start smoking pot right now. The occasional cigarette and drunk-off-my-butt weekend night or two are about all I can stomach of substance use. Plus, I'm not a huge fan of Jon becoming a pothead. He now has a poster of John Lennon surrounded by a plume of smoke above his headboard. I swear that wasn't there yesterday. Part of me wants to blame this on Sabita. After all, she's so new. But in my gut, I know this is Jon's choice.

After our mom died, Jon looked to me for everything —every morning before school, he'd say, *What should I wear?* I'd look out the window at the weather, and then describe the appropriate layering of apparel. He'd walk to his bedroom repeating the words, *short sleeves, long sleeves, pants.* And then he'd shout, *Undies? Yes,* I'd say. *Always undies, Jon. And socks!* For breakfast, I'd pour the milk for his cereal, or heat his instant oatmeal. I'm so used to him being a kid, my follower. But I guess everyone needs choices, even destructive ones. Jon can't stay in his box forever, playing lacrosse, cradling the silence.

And if anything, Jon is taking Sabita down with him. I like Sabita. I wonder what her parents would think of her dating a slightly older boy who buys and smokes pot. Then again, his sister gets drunk and randomly hooks up with boys on the weekends. We are winning.

"No, thanks," I say.

"Are you too good for our pot?" Jon says.

"Something like that."

"You're missing out."

I'm sure I am.

ME/JON

My brother is on a surfboard, but he's gone too far out. I'm watching him from the beach, feeling edgy about him being out there without me. And then the waves start getting bigger. Monstrosities of waves pounding into the surfers, flooding the beach. Jon disappears into wave after wave. I run into the water, but I can't get to him fast enough. Each wave is bigger than the one before it, and I'm being tossed around underwater, trying to find the surface so I can breathe, so I can get to Jon. But I'm alone. All I can see is sand and murky water, and bits of my hair tangling around my face. All I can think is, *There's no way Jon will survive this.*

I wake up with the momentary feeling of falling before the relief of the bed under my body floods me.

I hate that dream. I have it every few months, and it's terrifying. The worst part is knowing I'm supposed to be with Jon and having no way to get to him. I could save him if I could just get there faster. But the waves are merciless every time I have the nightmare.

I have a similar version of this dream, but it's a tsunami.

One big, earthshattering wave. I'm on the beach, and Jon is in the water with his board. When the water slams into my body, there's a split second of knowing that I might survive and he won't.

We've only been to the beach a few times. California. Jon took to surfing like he'd been doing it all his life. He's like that with sports. We were twelve and thirteen. I stood on the beach the whole time watching Jon, knowing that if something happened to him out there, I'd be too late. Anyone would be too late to get to him. He was on his own.

I stare at the ceiling. It's five a.m. Too early to get up and get ready for school. I finally fall asleep again right as my alarm goes off.

We came really close last night, me and Lance."

For a second I feel like I'm swimming. Marissa is talking, but I have no idea what she's saying because my head is underwater and I'm moving my arms and legs. She gets louder when I turn my head for air, but I want to go back under and turn her off. I thought I could do this, be there for her, but I'm not sure I can bear the weight of this with her. A make-out session that almost resulted in sex with Mr. Danson takes Marissa's flirtation to another level. No, another dimension.

"Dude," she says a second time.

"Dude," I repeat back. "He's married. He's a dad."

I say it because it's all I can think about, and being a good friend doesn't mean being all tra-la-la about how messed up this is.

"I know."

"And?"

"And I don't know. This is separate from that."

This is separate from that. That's how you can do this? By compartmentalizing? By thinking your actions aren't going to affect his marriage? I don't say it. My honesty has its limitations.

"It's not like I forced him. I kissed him and he kissed me back and we just kept kissing. And kissing. Things got out of hand because that's how uncontrollable it is. We got carried away. We are dynamite. Us *together*—together, it's inevitable."

I can see Mr. Danson and Marissa, their mouths and bodies desperate for each other.

I think my jaw is still on the floor, because she says, "He's a grown man with choices. And I'm a woman with choices. This is totally consensual, and he's gonna have to deal with his own life."

If this ever made headlines, Marissa would be painted as one of two things: a seductive, underdressed harlot or a wronged, innocent victim. Neither seems totally accurate, and yet she's both—part woman-seductress, part child-innocent. That word, *consensual.* It buzzes and hums in me until I can't stand it anymore.

"This isn't consensual, Marissa."

"What do you mean?" She folds her arms.

"By law, you can't *consent* to doing anything sexual with a teacher. He's in a position of power."

"Screw the law," she says. "He respects me. And I'm making this choice, okay?"

I look at this beautiful person I love so much, and all I see is a broken girl.

"I can't tell you it's okay," I say.

"Oh, and you pining over some guy with a girlfriend is okay?"

She's right. I never think about Maggie as someone who might love Tate; to me, she's just everything I'm not. I almost respond with *I can't help it*, but I realize those are the words she just used to describe this thing with Danson.

"This is different."

She folds her arms across her chest, eyes blazing into mine. "How? How is this different, Aden?"

"Tate and I are at least both teenagers. Mr. Danson is a full-grown adult."

I can see her body deflate, just, with my words. "Whatever, Aden. The feelings are the same. It's just reciprocated in my situation."

"Ouch, Marissa."

Marissa grabs her backpack off the floor, stuffs her books inside, and throws her hair into a messy bun. Then she looks at me with pity or apology before she quietly leaves my room.

JON

Sabita is stretched out on the basement couch, her feet resting on Jon's legs. Her hands are digging into a bowl of M&M's. She's methodically opening and closing her palm in the bowl, and the basement is eerily quiet except for the sound of Sabita's hand sifting in the candy.

I look at Jon, and something isn't quite right. "Jon?"

He raises his head slowly and smiles. Whoa, this smile is way too happy. This is not a marijuana high.

"Jon?" I say again, but I'm feeling a little panicked. "What did you take?"

He just laughs, but it's not a drunk laugh. It's a lucid-sounding laugh like I've said something clever and funny.

"You are a genius," he says. He's not really talking to me, though. We aren't connecting. "How could you know that I took something? That it isn't just pot?" He looks at Sabita. "How could she know that? Ade, have I ever told you how amazing you are?" He stands and puts both hands on my shoulders and looks into my eyes. I can't decide if I'm making eye contact with the devil who stole my brother's soul or if

I'm just connecting with some other side of him. It must be both. "Music. We need music. What the hell were we thinking? We don't have tunes!"

Sabita isn't here. She's in the bowl with those M&M's.

"Wow," she says. "I love M&M's in a bowl together. It's like touching heaven."

These two are so high. I've been so steeped in books and singing and surviving high school without a mom that I've never seen anyone this high. It's scary.

"Jon. What. Did. You. Take?"

He's humming to himself, messing with Dad's stereo from 1999. The music comes on loud, big band. Jon twirls around the room like a ballerina. I've entered an alternate universe.

"Ecstasy," he says. "And I finally know why it's called Ecstasy. But I can't figure out the whole Molly thing. If this was named after a person, Molly must've been incredible. Magnificent. Stupendous." He is totally ecstatic.

He grabs Sabita from the couch, and they start dancing together. Within seconds, they're full-body making out, and I hope to God she's on the pill or there's a condom down here.

I wonder how long Ecstasy lasts because my dad will be home in a few hours. I hope they don't have any more.

"Sabita, you should go home," I say, tapping her on the shoulder.

She turns her head and smiles as though she's just heard something pleasant.

"Jon. Sabita needs to go home."

"I can't send her home like this, Ade. Her parents would kill her."

"You're an idiot."

Jon laughs. "Go away, Aden."

"I don't like leaving you alone this way."

"I'm not alone." He buries his face in Sabita's hair. And for a split second, I think of Tate and wonder what it would feel like to be wanted enough by him that he would bury his nose in my hair, inhaling in ecstasy. High or not.

I shake the thought because it hurts and because I need to be present for Jon, and I head to the mini fridge we keep in the basement, grabbing two bottles of water, setting them on the table next to the M&M's. Reluctantly, I leave the two of them alone in the basement, leaning into each other, half dancing, half swaying, as though they're one thing.

When I check on them three hours later, Dad is home, grilling dinner, and Jon and Sabita are on the couch, half dressed, passed out.

"Come on, guys," I say. "Party's over. Sabita, get dressed. I think you should go home tonight."

She looks so sad. "Yeah, my parents were expecting me an hour ago."

I almost say, *I hope you don't get in trouble*, but realize that's ridiculous because she just did Ecstasy and God knows what with my brother.

I hand Sabita a water. She takes it as though it weighs a

hundred pounds. I've never seen her so lackluster. Seeing her now, coming down from Ecstasy, makes me realize how full of life and joy she is normally.

"Get the hell out of here, Aden!" Jon yells at me. It's unprovoked and like a shock of cold water in my face. I mentally regroup and realize this is the comedown. I know that the comedown can be harsh. Like being thrown into the depths of hell after a taste of heaven. At least that's what I read after I saw these two high and then went upstairs and Googled everything I could about Ecstasy.

"Jon, you're coming down from Ecstasy. This is what it feels like. You're gonna need to pull yourself together. Dad's home, and he wants to eat. Drink some water." I set a water bottle on the table next to him. "And eat some of those M&M's. Sugar and chocolate should do something for your endorphins."

I watch as Sabita gathers her clothes off the couch and starts relayering. She looks worse than I've ever seen her. Eyes glassy and clumped mascara. I think she might be crying.

Now I know what kind of underwear Sabita wears. Lacy. Underwear meant to be seen.

I exhale with a groan because I feel bad for Sabita and because I'm annoyed by their mess. I blame Jon for this; this is his undoing. And Sabita just happens to be in the line of fire.

I look at Jon and say slowly, enunciating every syllable, "This is the last time I cover for you. Don't do these kinds of drugs again." I want my words to sting. I'll say them again when he's sober.

He gives me one head nod, and I hope he's agreeing not to do it again, but I can't be sure.

I try to pick up the slack with the dinner conversation, but my dad notices Jon's foul mood.

"Everything okay?" Dad says.

"Hunky-dory." Jon is acting like a jerk. It's really out of character. I keep thinking about the wave dream.

"What's going on, Jon?" Dad starts to get red in the face. Anger—his default emotion. He takes everything personally.

"Jon and Sabita had a big fight," I say. I glare at Jon. His comedown is starting to make me mad, and if he lights Dad's fuse, I swear I'm going to lose it on him. I've been covering for him all afternoon, and in no way do I approve of him experimenting with party drugs.

"Yeah," Jon says. "Sorry. Is it okay if I take the rest of this up to my room?"

Dad heaves a long sigh. "Do what you will."

"Should I be worried?" he says after Jon leaves.

"Maybe."

ME

It's the D-string. My mom's guitar is in decent shape save the D-string, which is broken. I play anyway. But every chord needs the D. My hands move from C to F and back again, pretending the D is intact.

I wonder if I'm invoking her spirit by playing her guitar after the many years it's sat untouched.

I'm picturing my mother in an ambulance, oxygen mask over her mouth, this stupid guitar underneath the gurney.

I'm singing Joni Mitchell's "Blue." It's about sinking or sailing away. It's about empty spaces in our hearts and filling them with all the wrong things. My voice cracks over the words. I let go and sing. This letting go and my cracking voice fill the space between me and my mom.

I cry. I sing and I cry and I play the guitar. In my mind I see flashes of my mom, and all the moments she's missed since she died. All the moments she should've seen, heard, and felt. All the times when she should've been my mom.

When I finish the last note, I look up from my guitar and there's Dad standing in the doorway.

I can't remember the last time he was in my room, but he crosses the threshold with ease, and before I know it, he's sitting next to me, one arm wrapped around my shoulder, and I'm leaning into him, crying. He smells of sawdust and deodorant. It's the smell of bike rides, bruised knees, and cuddles. I can't remember the last time I let him hold me.

I think my dad is crying too. But I'm afraid to know even though I know. Because seeing him break might ruin the illusion that I'm safe. And for a split second, here in my dad's arms, I have everything I need.

But this? This is so far from okay. And yet it is. I have to be okay without my mom because I *am* without her. It's messed up, but I take solace in the fact that we're without her together. Me, Dad, Jon. It's never just us. It's us minus one.

den. Hello? Earth to Aden . . ." It's my English teacher. She's asked me a question, and I'll be darned if I know what we're even talking about. I was thinking about Mr. Danson and Marissa. Lance Danson. Mister Danson.

"Sorry," I say. "I really wasn't paying attention. I'm tuned in now."

"Thanks for joining us."

Why are high school teachers always as snarky as their students?

I wonder how and where it's finally going to happen. The sex. In a hotel? In a janitor's closet somewhere after school? Should I tell someone? Who would I tell?

I have to talk to Marissa one more time.

JON

*J*on sits on his bed, eyes closed, hands crossed over his flat belly. Abs. I should call his midsection abs. He looks alarmingly like my dad. Minus the belly. His posture is all too familiar, filled with grief and shame.

"Jon?" He's silent. "What's going on?"

I sit on his bed, scooting back to lean on the headboard. I push my feet into his legs.

"Come on, Jon. Something's up."

He looks up at me with red eyes. "I screwed up, Ade."

"What'd you do?"

The eyes are disconcerting. I'm not sure if he's high or if he's been crying. Either way, I'm afraid of what's behind these red eyes.

"Drugs."

"Drugs?"

"Well, just the pot."

"I think you should stop smoking, Jon. It just doesn't seem like this whole pot-smoking thing is going anywhere good."

"I am, Ade. I'm stopping. But I got caught buying from Max Steele in the hall today."

We pause. A mutual break in the conversation while we both take in that Jon got caught buying marijuana on our high school campus.

This might change everything for him. He could lose his spot on the lacrosse team—which means no sports scholarship. Not to mention how Dad must've reacted. "Does Dad know?"

"Yeah. We met with Dean Chan. In the middle of the school day. Dad had to leave work, drop me at home, and go back to work."

My face must say it all.

"Yeah," he says. "I know. What do I do?"

"I don't know. Did they tell you what's going to happen?"

"They called the cops. Three-day suspension and possible possession charges."

"Wow."

Part of me wants to be mad at Jon for making such a stupid decision. I know he can do better than this. But then I think of him and Dad arguing in the hallway and him up late studying and him loving Sabita. He's needed something more, a mom, for a long time. I wish I could change everything and make his world a place where only light and love exist. I hate that I can't do that for him.

"Now what?"

"I don't know, Ade. I did it. I'm an idiot. I tried to buy pot in the halls at Bentley."

"So that happened." I pause, searching his face for recognition, for acceptance of that fact. "You can't go back in time. Neither of us can. So we have to find some way to float this."

We. Are we in this together?

"I'm not sure I know how. My whole life is about to crash into the ground." His eyes are welling. "And Dad." They're spilling tears now. "He can't even look at me, Aden."

The Dad part. It's the worst part. Jon's spent so much of his childhood trying to make Dad proud, and he just murdered his lacrosse career. Lacrosse is where Dad shows pride in Jon.

I scoot next to him on the bed and pull him into my chest. Like he's a little boy. And then he *is* a little boy, crying into my shirt. My heart is in pieces. I wonder if this is what it feels like to be a mom. We both know she should be the one here, doing the holding. But she's not and I am, and sometimes I love my brother like a mom might.

He pulls away and grabs some tissues off his desk, balling them into his fists after he blows his nose.

"You'll find a way to float," I say. "Life may look different, but there's another side."

Jon looks at me with his little-boy face and exhales. "How do you know?"

"Well, life is full of this kind of stuff, right? You're not the only boy who ever got caught with drugs at Bentley. This isn't a death sentence. So, yeah, there's always an other side, and maybe, just maybe, you'll come out better."

Everything I'm saying sounds so cliché, but I believe it. I have to. This is my little brother.

"You sound like a self-help book," he says.

"You sound like a kid who tried Ecstasy and only got caught buying pot. Don't get sassy."

"I'm gonna lie down for a while," he says.

There's a distance in his tone that I can't cross. So I leave his room, the door open a crack so he's not completely alone.

DAD

I've avoided him for the last twenty-four hours. I wonder what he's thinking. If he's ashamed.

I sit down next to him on the porch without saying anything. I try to relax my breathing as I wait for my dad to say something.

"What, Ade?" He's gruff but not ragey.

"I dunno. Are you okay?"

He releases a breath. It's a long time before he answers. "I don't know. Is Jon?"

"I don't know."

Another long pause. "I just thought . . ."

I'm not sure he's going to finish his thought. I'm not sure he wants to have this conversation.

"You just thought?"

"I didn't mean to make light of his pot smoking. If it's a problem. I didn't know he'd be an idiot."

"I know," I say. "I didn't think he'd be that stupid about it either."

"Have there been any other drugs, Aden?"

The question throws me. I take a minute to collect myself, and I wonder if he knows because I've taken too long to answer.

"Please don't make me say it out loud, Dad. Jon might never forgive me."

"How bad is it, Ade?"

I curse myself for betraying Jon, but right now he needs protection from himself more than he needs protection from consequences. "So far a one-off. Experimental. But will you ask him about it? I want him to trust me."

My dad rubs his forehead, distressed. "Fine, I won't ask for more information. But if he doesn't provide me with every little detail, I'm coming for you."

I nod once. I'll tell him if I have to, all of it.

"Did you do drugs when you were younger, Dad?"

"It was the eighties."

"What does that mean?"

"I tried a few."

"And you turned out okay, right?"

He squints at me. "Debatable."

I laugh. "You think Jon'll be okay?"

"If I know my son."

"So now what?" I say.

"Who knows?" My dad's fingers are pressed between his brows like he's trying to rub out the creases.

He looks at me, and the pain I see in his eyes is a shocking jolt.

"What, Dad?"

"You think he's serious about this Rhode Island School of Design thing?"

"I do."

He sighs. "A full ride. A chance to play sports in college. He was so passionate about lacrosse." He shakes his head, "And two private school tuitions. I'm not sure I can do it, and your mom . . ."

"What about Mom?"

"Never mind, Aden."

"Dad?" I think of Jon and the weed and the Ecstasy and RISD, and I say, "Who cares what mom would've wanted? She's not here. We are. And we're going to have to figure something out." *Because I'm not giving up Brandeis.* I don't say that last bit out loud. But it's true. And I will say it. Just not now.

I think my dad is going to say something else, but instead his hands move to his belly, and he crosses them there, closing his eyes.

I'm in my room, trying to work out this song. The feeling of it, the melody, it's all here. But the words . . . It's like I can't quite reach them.

> *What is beauty?*
> *It's just love.*
> *Beautiful is the space between*
> *Everything I've known and*
> *Everything I know now*
>
> *What is love?*
> *It's knowing.*
> *~~It's recognizing each other's~~*
> *Souls*

I don't know if Tate can't love me because I'm not beautiful like Maggie, or if he can't love me because I'm not Maggie. Or if it's something else. But it's just when I start to think Tate can't love me that I think maybe he can. Or does.

I know it's not that I'm not beautiful, period. Everyone is beautiful somehow. Mostly, I'm driving myself crazy. I think about the last time Tate and I sat at Ike's together and the crack in his armor. Followed by Maggie's entrance. Invasion, really. The truth is, I can't control any of it.

MARISSA

"Don't do this," I say, my hand on Marissa's forearm, tugging at her, trying to get her to see me, to see what I'm saying.

She pulls away. "Stop being so dramatic, Ade. Jesus."

"I'm not being dramatic, Marissa. This is a horrible idea."

"Keep your voice down." We're standing at her locker, whisper-yelling. The bell rang minutes ago, and we're both late for class. I don't care, because Marissa has plans to meet Danson tonight in some random parking lot, and my insides are screaming and I'm talking as quietly as I possibly can but I will explode if I don't stop this from happening.

"Listen, Marissa. Flirting is one thing. But this? This is a whole new level of wrong."

"Shhh." She's shushing me loudly, hissing, really. "This is happening." She puts a hand on my shoulder, sighs impatiently, and looks into my eyes. "I swear to you, Aden. I know what I'm doing, okay? I'm fine. Promise."

"You're not fine. This is not fine."

"So what are you going to do about it?"

"Should I tell someone?" It comes out as a question because I'm deeply conflicted. The naivety in me actually believes that Marissa has control, that she's owning herself and her sexuality in making this choice. The adult in me knows that she's not empowered in this choice; in fact it's just the opposite.

Now Marissa is whisper-yelling when she says, "Don't you dare, Aden. I will never speak to you again."

"So what?" I say, even though I don't mean it. The thought of not speaking to Marissa is a gash I can't imagine. "This is what loving someone looks like. I can't always tell you what you want to hear."

"Oh, get off your high horse, Aden. Clearly, you don't know the first thing about love. Or should I say, about someone loving you back."

She slams her locker shut and walks away.

I clutch my stomach. Her words ripped into the core of me.

ME

I see Mr. Danson from the hall the day after he and Marissa finally have sex in the back of his minivan. Or, at least, I assume they did. Marissa and I haven't spoken since our fight.

A female student leans over him while he marks her paper. I think she's *leaning* leaning, but I'd assume that about any female student of Danson's at this point. I wonder if Mr. Danson will have sex with her in the back of the van, too. Was the car seat there, or did he take that out to make more room?

Marissa thinks she loves him. I wonder how she can love a man, a dad, who cheats on his wife with a seventeen-year-old student.

I watch Danson as though we're in a slow-motion time warp. He alternates between looking at his student and looking down at the paper they're both intently studying.

I'll never look at him the same way again.

And to think I once found him inspiring.

SETH

I'm stuck. I'm so afraid to move. I'm so afraid to break what I have with Tate because I love him so much I could explode. But where we are is drowning me, moment by moment. I'm stuck and lost. Marissa and I are back on speaking terms, pretending we never fought, but we both know there's a canyon between us. I couldn't save her, even though I tried. Didn't I? And Jon. I can't help him because, God, you can't save people from themselves. My insides are volcanic, but I still have to walk around every day like everything is okay.

Instead of telling Tate I love him and demanding more because how can he not see that we're perfect together, or simply exploding and shattering everywhere, I get ready for Ryan's party with Marissa. We pregame in my room because the party's only a few blocks away. I'm acting like a moron, but I don't care. I guess I'm a girl who "pregames" now.

Three shots in, and I make it tonight's goal to get Seth alone. At least he'll have me *like that*. It's messed up, I know, but everything hurts so much, and I have to find a way to make it feel better. Sober me knows this isn't the way to do it, but drunk me loves that Seth Bernum wants me in a sexual way, a way I'm not sure Tate has ever fathomed wanting me.

Ryan's party is at least in a normal house in a normal neighborhood. No beautiful moms with baskets of car keys or surround sound or a full bar. Just a house with old carpet and a bunch of kegs. We walked here.

"What's up?" Marissa says, slinging a sloppy arm around my shoulder.

"What's up with you?"

I'm not the only one cocooning. Marissa's had twice as much to drink as I have, and she's the size of my pinky toe. She doesn't seem to be slowing down.

"Just keeping up with the Joneses." She uses her sleeve to wipe vodka from her chin. At least we're equal parts disaster tonight.

I have no idea how we make it to Ryan's, because Marissa and I are completely drunk. Seth is in the kitchen with his crew. We make eye contact across the room, and he points his thumb upstairs.

I stumble to the stairs and crawl my way up. I take a minute to feel the carpet rub between my fingers, vaguely aware of how weird it is to do that.

Seth is behind me pushing me forward. Jeez, he's eager. It's like getting groped at a sleazy club. I'm not ready for anything having to do with his pelvis just yet, but he's pushing his hips into mine. His breath is hot on my neck. Everything is duller around the edges, and Seth is breaching my boundaries. At least he wants me. *Like that.*

The walls are a hazy mess of lavender and pink. Everything is fuzzy, and Seth is moving way too fast. His hand is up my skirt, and I'm trying to push it down, but he's not getting the message.

"Whoa, whoa, whoa, cowboy. Slow down."

He puts his knee between my legs, shoving it into my crotch as he lifts himself off me to see my face.

"What, you don't want this?"

His knee is pressing too hard. No, I don't want this, but it's Seth Bernum. I'm supposed to want him if I'm any kind of a girl. But somewhere in me I know this isn't how it's supposed to feel.

"Just slow down. Can we kiss for a minute?"

"Sure," he says.

We're slobbering again, but his hands are roaming everywhere, and did he just dribble beer into my cleavage? I stare at the walls trying to find some semblance of clarity, but I feel so dizzy.

This is not what I want. This is not what I want. This is not what I want. He eases off me.

I think Seth is unbuttoning his jeans and I think I'm lying under him on the bed but how can I be sure when alcohol has turned the world into sheer haze? Where are my words? Where are my words?

"Seth, no. Stop."

He laughs.

"Seriously Seth, stop. We're not having sex tonight, okay? Stop."

I'm pushing him off, but suddenly he's pressing his whole body against me, rubbing up and down my leg.

"Don't get cold feet, Aden. This is why we came up here."

He's breathing hot beer breath into my ear. I'm repulsed. Seth wants something and I'm drunk, but I know enough to know it's not *me* he wants.

"Get. Off me."

His hands are under my skirt again, fiddling with my panties.

"Just let me make you feel good, okay?" he says. "I swear you'll change your mind."

I'm so drunk. I forget my resolve. The room is spinning. Seth is doing something to me. His hands are roaming my body. My clothes are wet, and I think it's beer or slobber or some bodily fluid. I forget. Seth Bernum.

Wait. No. No. It doesn't feel good. This doesn't feel good. His fingers are thick and clumsy, and everything about this hurts. It hurts.

He's not listening, and I'm too weak and too drunk to push him off. He has one hand on a breast. I wish I wasn't under him. I need to not be under him, and I wish the room would just stop spinning for one second.

"Me on top," I say.

He looks surprised, but lets me flip out from under him and start to straddle him.

Instead I stumble for the door, taking the spinning room and a blanket with me as I go. I'm still drunk, half dressed, and my hand slips and he grabs my other arm.

"Not so fast, Aden."

I manage to push the door open and there are people sitting right outside the door smoking and drinking and laughing and I'm so relieved.

Seth is trying to pull me back into the room, but I lock eyes with a girl from my history class. What's her name? What on earth is her name?

"Sara. Sara, hi."

She starts talking to me and Seth pulls me backwards.

"Stop." I say it loud and firm in front of everyone, and there's nothing he can do but let me go.

I'm sober and drunk and sad and I think I'm crying and I can't find Marissa because she left with Josh. I have to get out of here so I stumble away with no shirt and someone else's coat thrown over my shoulder. Who put a coat on me?

"Where are you?" Tate's voice on the phone.

"I don't know. I'm lost. I'm in my neighborhood. I'm lost. I don't know where I am."

I think I'm talking too loudly into the phone.

"Breathe, Ade," he says. "Are you at Ryan's party?"

"Yes. I mean, no. I was. I'm outside." I feel so incoherent. I'm not sure I'm making any sense.

"Okay. Sit down. Right where you are. Can you do that?"

"Yes." I sit.

"In the grass. Not the street. Just sit down and stay put.

Got it?" Tate is talking to me as though I'm a five-year-old. But it's exactly what I need right now.

"Ade? Are you still with me?"

"I'm here."

"Stay on the phone."

"Okay." I lie down and look up at the night's fuzzy sky. The whole sky, stars and all, spins around me. I close my eyes.

"Ade. Ade. Wake up."

Tate is leaning over me. His hand on my shoulder. I think he's brushing the hair from my face.

"Can you walk?"

He's pulling me up from the . . . grass? All I want to do is close my eyes and go to sleep.

"Aden." Tate's voice is like silk wrapping itself around me. It's warm. I want to sleep in the warmth of Tate's voice.

Tate pulls me into his arms. He has to crouch to support my weight.

"Aden. Come on."

"You know I love you, right?"

"I know, Ade."

"I want to be with you." I'm burying my face into his chest. He smells like pine and sleep. It's so warm here.

"You are with me. I'm here."

"No. I'm in love with you. I want to be with you."

"We can't talk about this right now. You're drunk."

"When, Tate? When we can we talk about it?"

I can feel the hysteria of loving him, wanting him, the frustration of every feeling I have for him spilling out of me.

Tate eases me into the passenger seat of a car. His mom's? He doesn't answer, but lets out a long breath as he reaches around my torso and buckles my seat belt. I reach for his face with my uncooperative, drunk hand, and run my fingers along his cheekbone, my hands grazing the stubble along his jaw-line. He puts his hand over mine and gently moves it to his chest, squeezing, looking into my eyes.

We are both sober, seeing each other's souls.

* * *

When I wake, I'm in my bra and skirt, a foreign, unfamiliar-smelling coat draped over me. I'm on the couch in my own house. When last night's events come flooding back, I pull the coat over my face and groan.

Seth.

Tate. The part about Tate. And loving him. And was I confessing my love in only my bra? The memory of his smell and touching his face, and his hand around mine—our hands together on his chest—it all makes my stomach rise to my throat, and I run to the bathroom and vomit—more than once.

It's dawn, and no one in my house is awake. I crawl up the stairs, discard the coat and my skirt on the floor, and go to sleep in my own bed.

ME

Noon. I want to close my eyes and wake up as someone else. I wish I wish I wish last night never happened. Tate's song, "No Regrets," rings in my head. Yeah, well, he's never acted like a slut and been finger raped all in one night. Regret. There is no word strong enough for the filth I feel everywhere.

I pull myself up to lean against my headboard. Waking up is the worst part. Shower. Get dressed. Coffee. I can do these things. I grab my robe and head for the bathroom. This shower is a thousand times worse than the shower I took at Alex's. The shame won't drain. I use all the imagination I can muster, but this shame is sticky like honey. Polluted honey. The water just rushes over and around it. I wonder why I keep making the same stupid mistakes.

I tie my hair back without brushing it and put on the baggiest sweats I can find. Nothing is right. I burn the toast. The coffee isn't hot enough.

There's one unread message on my phone. I'm lucky the

phone is still in my possession after last night. I'll probably never see my suede jacket again.

Morning-after pill. Come get me?

I grab the keys, my phone, my wallet, my coffee, and my awful tasting toast and head for the door.

10 min.

There's a free walk-in clinic, but it's downtown. It'll take us half an hour to get there.

Marissa opens the door to my car and gets in. No eye contact. No greeting. She folds her hands over the top of her giant purse. I reach over and squeeze a hand, and before she can reject my affection, I put the car in reverse and we're on our way.

She nudges her head in the direction of a drive-thru Starbucks off the highway. I get a giant mocha with whip, and she her black coffee.

"So, Josh?" *Please don't be Danson. Please don't be Danson.*

"Yeah." I wonder if she's lying.

"I thought you weren't into him like that."

"Well, apparently I changed my mind last night."

"You're entitled. What about . . ." I pause. I want to say Mr. Danson, but he doesn't deserve that kind of respect. "Lance?"

"It's over."

"It is?"

"Yeah. Happy?"

"God, yes."

Her eyes well with tears.

"You really cared about him," I say, trying to soften the blow of my relief.

"So much, Aden."

"How did it end?"

"We met up twice last week and, you know, had sex. We used condoms. Maybe I texted him too many times or something. But he sent me a text that said he loves his wife and we have to stop."

I can't tell if she feels shame or regret. She's so much more . . . muted than usual. Crushed. And then it dawns on me. It's not shame or regret. What she feels is unloved. Or unlovable. I know those feelings.

I reach for her hand, and limply, she reaches for mine. I squeeze tightly before I have to reach for the stick shift again.

I think of poor, foolish Josh and how much he cares for Marissa, despite how she uses him. She could do worse than Josh. Like Mr. Danson worse than Josh. But I don't say it. I think some part of her knows.

Josh's thing for Marissa started when she moved here in second grade. I think it's sweet. I don't know what Marissa thinks. She keeps him around. My guess is she doesn't know she deserves a guy like Josh. She doesn't know she doesn't know. It's messed up. The two of us are some pair.

"I thought I heard something about you and Seth again last night?"

She's changing the subject. We're not talking about going

to a clinic to get the morning-after pill because she had sex and having sex can make you pregnant. We'll pretend like it's no big deal, but we both know it is.

"Yeah. Something." I say.

"And? This doesn't sound like a good something."

Despite my resolve, my eyes well with tears, and I tell her everything as I alternate wiping my tears and keeping my hands on the steering wheel and stick shift. The driving helps me, because I'm in control when I'd otherwise be spinning out completely. I tell her about how drunk and fuzzy I was. About how he kept pressing his hips into me and breathing all over my neck and how I thought him wanting me was supposed to be cool.

"Oh, Aden," she says. She tucks some loose hair behind my ear in the most compassionate gesture. I cry again, wiping my tears quickly because the light we'd stopped at changes from red to green.

"It's going to be okay," she says. "Now you know he's the guy you thought he was, right?"

I laugh through my tears.

"He's so much worse, Marissa."

She sighs. "People have such a way of letting us down, don't they?"

"Yeah," I say. "Not that my expectations for Seth Bernum were all that high. But my expectations for my first make-out session were through the roof. So there's that letdown."

"This one doesn't count. You'll get your first good one. I promise. It can be better."

I don't know why, but I can't bring myself to tell Marissa about the Tate part of my night. That he came and got me. That I buried my face in his chest and told him that I'm in love with him.

The pill costs Marissa thirty dollars. She doesn't have enough cash, so I throw in ten bucks of babysitting money. She swallows the pill with her cold coffee. Her face is sad and worried. I wonder if this is what shame feels like for her.

"This better work," she says.

"We need comfort food." I say. "Greasy diner or donuts?"

"Greasy diner," she says.

"Good choice." And I squeeze her hand again. She squeezes back.

JON

I'm off the team."

He's lying on his bed, an arm over his face.

"What?"

"I'm off the team, Aden. No mercy. No bench. Just done. I knew this could happen. That it would probably happen, but it feels so final. I feel like an outcast. The guys won't even talk to me."

My brother isn't brainless. He knew what he was risking.

"In a way, though, isn't this what you wanted? A break?"

"I didn't know it would be like this."

I think he's crying, but he won't let me see his face.

"Maybe they just need time, Jon. They're probably feeling a little let down, right?"

"Yeah. I guess."

I sit down on the edge of his bed. He's still not looking at me.

"What about next year?"

"What about it?"

"Maybe there's a chance you can play next year?"

He looks up, finally taking the arm off his red, wet face. "I don't know, Ade. I'm not sure I want back on the team. But Dad has a scout lined up for every game."

Our eyes meet, his so swollen and so full of uncertainty.

"I'm sorry about the scholarship. I know you were counting on it, too," he says.

I put my hand on his arm. "But I shouldn't have been. I'm sorry for adding to all the pressure. It's been way too much. I'll figure it out." I silently promise myself that if I get in, I'll find a way to go to Brandeis. I'll do what it takes.

"Dad." The arm goes back over his face because he's crying again. We're talking about Dad. "He only speaks to me in one-word sentences. It's like he can't even stand to be around me. He's ashamed of me, Aden."

"He'll get over it. I promise. Dads don't stay ashamed of their sons. That's just not how it works."

"Is that what you think, Jon?" Dad is standing in the doorway. "That I'm ashamed of you?" His voice is soft.

Jon nods.

Dad comes in and sits next to Jon on the bed. He starts to say something, and we're both waiting for whatever comes out of his mouth to take the weight off of us, if even for a moment. "I just . . ." But he pauses without continuing, and the silence that follows is thick, a barrier between us and him.

"I'm sorry I'm off the team, Dad."

"I'm sorry you are, too, son. It's not shame." He searches for the words. "It's . . ."

We wait.

Finally he says, "Sadness," with such finality it feels as if he's sapped the air out of the room.

Then, he pats Jon on the shoulder, lingering in the doorway before he leaves the room.

My brother's tears can't be controlled. I can't save him from this heartbreak.

SABITA

*S*he's sitting on the step of our front porch when I pull into the driveway. It's no wonder she's a sculptor. She is art. It's not just in her beauty, though there is that. I think it's in her soul. Expressed in her body. If I weren't so jealous of her, I might have my own crush. That would be weird.

Her face is sad. I have no idea what's going on between her and my brother. I make my way toward the front door. Toward Sabita. She stands and brushes flaked leaves off her white sweater.

"Jon's watching practice today," I say. "Hoping to get a word in with his coach and some of the guys afterward."

"Oh," she says.

This is awkward.

And after a beat, she adds, "That's good."

It strikes me that she might not know what's good for my brother. What does she know of him? I think about the intimacy I've caught between them. The knowing glances, accidentally walking in on them, bodies intertwined. And then I have to admit that in some ways she knows more of him than I do.

"Yeah. I'm not sure it'll do any good, but I don't suppose he can make things much worse for himself."

Sabita is blocking my path to the door, and I'm not sure if she wants to stay an hour and wait for him or go home.

"I didn't know he was going to do it."

"What?"

"Buy pot. At school. I didn't know. I didn't even know where he was getting the weed. It was his third time buying. I pitched in a few bucks. I guess I didn't want to know where or how he was getting it."

"Yeah," I say, feeling a little angry at her for being Jon's accomplice in all this. "Well, now you know."

She sighs. "Yeah. Now I know."

Her eyes are so sad. And huge—framed by dark, long lashes. And even though I'm trying to believe she's simply young and pretty, uninspiring, every time I look at her, I see so much. I sigh.

"Want to come in? I'm starving."

"Yeah, if it's okay."

"Yes, it's okay. I'm sure Jon will want someone to talk to after his meeting."

Letting go. I'm letting go of the fact that Jon will want to talk to Sabita and not me.

"Do you think it'll be okay with your dad? I mean, do you think he's mad at me?"

"Honestly, I don't know what's okay with my dad these days."

MAGGIE

*M*aggie. It's not that I think she's better than
me. If anything, maybe it's the opposite. It would be easy to
characterize her as the shallow cheerleader type who gets the
guy and me as the girl next door who pines after the guy. Eventually the guy will realize what he's had all along, and he'll pick
me. But that's not life. Life is that she's here and I'm here, and
I'm in love with her boyfriend. And we're both people.

She's waiting for me outside the door of our choir room.
Her gun is loaded, I can tell. Finger on the trigger. I'm totally
unarmed. I think I must always be unarmed.

She strides in next to me, steps perfectly in sync with
mine. The *click-click* of her heels is the only sound before she
says, "I know everything. I just thought you should know."
Click-click, click-click, click-click, as she walks away.

I think about Tate talking to Maggie about me, and it
dawns on me that she probably knows exactly how Tate feels
about me. Or, if not exactly, she certainly has a better idea
than I do.

Bang.

*I*n math, Tate walks down the aisle to the pencil sharpener. On the way to his desk he brushes his hand across my back. I can smell his morning shower and something sweet. Do they make body spray for men?

He knows I love him.

After class we both put our coats and backpacks on, and without talking, we walk to Ike's for free period. He buys our coffees again and two donuts, and carries them to our spot. We have a spot.

He's trying to make this less awkward, but I don't think I can pretend like nothing's happened. I can't pretend that I haven't told him I love him. And that now he holds the truth, and he's acting like everything should be the same between us. As though I'll just be me and he'll just be him and we'll go on and on with me loving him and him knowing. He knows my soul. I don't know his. Does he think he can keep having me just as I am? And Maggie just as she is? Reality will stay just like this and I'll keep loving him and giving my light to him and he'll glow even brighter because of it. It's a cold truth that maybe he'll never return that light.

"I'm sorry I was such a drama queen the other day." It's not what I want to say, but I can't find the words because, in truth, I'm so afraid I'll change everything with one sentence said soberly, in the light of day. And if everything changes, then Tate can't have me like this and maybe I can't have what little he gives me of him either. When he's all I want. And sometimes I convince myself that if we can't be together *like that*, then I'll take what I can get despite the pain.

"I have no idea what you're talking about."

What if I just let it lie? Maybe I should just turn myself off and go back to numbers. I'm good at numbers.

"You know what I'm talking about."

The problem is, math is really lonely.

He sighs. He knows I'm taking us there whether he likes it or not.

"It's done. Don't worry about it," he says. He looks down at his calculus textbook. He's on page fifty-three. Our homework is on page fifty-six. I watch him stare at the page with creased eyebrows until I finally reach over and flip the pages for him. He looks at me.

"So, you think I'm a slut?" I mean to say *I love you* again, so that he'll know it was me talking that night and not the alcohol. I should've said it, but fear is choking me, holding the words hostage.

"You know what I think of you." He puts his head in his hands. "You can do so much better than him, Ade."

I don't know what he thinks of me. There it is. This assumption that I should somehow know exactly where I stand with Tate. His words ignite something in me. There's no going back.

"Really? Because he's, like, the most popular guy in school." My tone is a dart. I pause. "And for the record, I have no idea what you think of me." I spit the words.

I wish he would just say it. That he doesn't or couldn't ever *love me like that.*

I'm on the brink of begging him to say it.

"So whatever. He's the most popular guy in school. He can go fuck himself. Popularity's not everything. I can't believe we're even talking about this. The guy's also the biggest jerk I know. You should . . ." He trails off. He sounds really invested. He sounds angry. And I wonder where he gets off acting like a jealous boyfriend when he's not that.

"I should what?"

"Hear the way he talks about you."

The idea that Tate has heard Seth talking about me *like that* is acid in my stomach rising to my throat.

"I'd prefer not to, thanks."

"So why'd you do it?"

"I don't know, Tate. Why are you asking?"

"Because I care about you, Aden. Isn't that obvious?"

I want to say it so badly. Here. Both of us really sober. It's on the tip of my tongue, about to roll out of my mouth and knock him over. Forever changing whatever this is.

"I'm in love with you, Tate. There. I said it in plain

daylight. I'm not drunk. Who cares what I did or didn't do with Seth Bernum, because I'm in love with you." Now it's out there. Maybe I've ruined everything, but I can't do this anymore. My breath is roped to my stomach, suspended mid-air. We're silent, and I'm not sure I remember how to breathe, because here it comes. The part where Tate puts me out of my misery. The part where our "fast friendship" ends, because who can hold this much love without hating it or returning it?

Tate doesn't break eye contact with me. His eyes are murky in this light.

"Your turn."

"My turn for what, Ade? I'm in a relationship with Maggie. You know this."

"I know," I say. "But tell me this isn't real."

I'm on the brink of tears. Maybe this thing with Tate is in my head after all. Maybe whatever he says next makes me feel like the fool that I am.

His inhale is sharp. "I don't have to. This"—he grabs both of my hands—"is real."

His words are a shocking validation. Painful and liberating.

"I want more," I say.

"I know." He's still holding my hands and I'm afraid to break eye contact because I know that when I do, this moment will be over and I'll wonder if it was a dream.

DAD

*C*upboards. Doors. Tools. Everything is crashing in the basement. It's thunder. It's rage. I hate this. It's been four days since Jon was caught on campus buying weed, and we've been waiting for the fallout. Except Jon isn't home. I am.

I weigh my options, knowing I could avoid this and let him do what he always does—rage, sulk, rinse, repeat. But I think we both know we need a change.

I stand at the foot of the stairs and listen to him. He's swearing, saying awful, awful things. As I stand there listening to him, I'm drawn to the heat of his temper, and momentarily, I want to join him. My stomach twists into a knot, my father's anger shaking me. God, it would feel so good to throw something and watch it shatter.

I find a time to swing the door to his workroom open in between crashes and swears.

Breathe. "Dad?"

"What, Aden?"

"Is everything okay?" It's a stupid question, I know. I

realize I didn't have a plan coming down here—I just couldn't keep avoiding him, his anger, or whatever's underneath it.

My dad looks around the room. He's made a mess. He tosses a screw into a box and sits down on the cement floor, my presence deflating him. He's a big man, my dad. But he looks so like a little boy, crumpled on the cement floor of his workroom.

"Is this about Jon, Dad?"

He looks up at me and then shakes his head, not in disagreement, but like I couldn't possibly understand.

I push on him. "Is it?"

"I guess so," he says finally, the words having let the remaining air out of his fury.

"Why are you so angry?" I know the question is loaded.

"I don't . . ." His voice trails off and our eyes meet, his head still heavy, but cocked as if a question has just formed in his head.

"What?"

"It's just . . ." He chuckles low and soft. And when he says, "I'm not sure it's anger," I understand why he's laughed without humor. We both know it's time to stop calling all of his feelings anger, even if that's how they're expressed.

"What is it, then?"

He shrugs. He doesn't have the right word yet.

"Dad, are you worried about Jon?"

He nods once because that's it. My dad is so worried about Jon.

"Me too." Even though it doesn't fix anything, there's relief in naming the truth. "What were you looking for?"

"My wrench. The one with the red handle."

"Oh. Want me to help?"

He grunts in lieu of answering. I look under a table against the wall and find it immediately. I wonder how long it took him to blow a gasket on this.

I hand him the wrench, and he takes it, slumped in defeat. "What were you working on, Dad?" I realize I haven't asked him about his project in months. His last big project, a horse commissioned by a hardware store customer, is gone.

For the first time since I've been in my dad's space, we look at each other. He motions his head in the direction of his smaller worktable.

On the table sits half of a silver watch, taken apart, the small gears and wheels piled together next to the actual project. As I study the pieces of silver and other metal that have been melted and pieced together, I see it. It's a music note pendant, about two inches in length, the insides of the watch decorating it.

"What . . ." I start to say.

"Graduation present." He's tired now. "The watch was your mom's."

Without looking at me again, he starts collecting the tools on the floor, putting them back in their large box.

"I'm going to love it."

He gives me a half smile, but his eyes look lighter. I stand in the doorway for a second, watching him put things away, thinking how much easier it is to mask sadness with fury, but how much more it costs.

ME and TATE

*T*hey say timing is everything. I'm not sure it's everything, but it must be something. Like meeting Tate. When I'm this and he's that. But here we are. Me and him and Maggie and Marissa and Jon. My dad. Here we all are just trying to hold it together enough to make it through tomorrow a little more gracefully than yesterday. At least that's what I'm trying to do. It won't get better or more graceful or even different unless I make it so.

I think about Tate and the way I ripped open my heart a few weeks ago and showed him the contents. I told him I loved him. And he didn't run or cringe, or even pull away; we've carried on, the electricity sparking and snapping between us. He can hold so much of me without rejecting me, but can he love me? It burns that he won't show me more of him, but I'm starting to think that maybe there's room for change.

So tonight will be different. I will be different.

Tonight it snows. The kind of snow that silences everything it touches. I'm grateful for the hush. I'm grateful for the early arrival of darkness.

I wrap a red scarf around my neck before leaving to get Tate. The night and the red and the snow make me feel beautiful. Tonight it snows and I'm beautiful.

Even though I love Tate, there's this part of me that is starting to hate him. But I love him much more than I actually hate him, so I let myself go to him. I let myself make this mistake again and again and again. It's become a way of being cruel to myself. It's a way of getting my fix. But it's never enough. Tate is my addiction.

When I pull into Tate's drive and flash my lights, the door opens and he runs out barefoot, wearing jeans and a sweater that makes his eyes the color of the storm clouds. I roll down the window.

"Come in," he says. "My mom just made a batch of hot cocoa."

"Cocoa?" He sounds like a three-year-old, but he's running back to the house, and I have no choice but to turn the car off and follow.

Tate's mom is warm and laughing and light, like she was at the coffee shop, like Tate. Tate's dad is working at the hospital, noticeably absent.

For a minute, as I watch his mom move around the house in a warm fleece bathrobe, serving us hot chocolate in thick, artsy mugs, I let myself imagine she's my mom. But I don't linger there, because I don't really want Mrs. Newman to be my mom. I want my mom to be my mom.

She tells me to call her Sandy, and so I do. She turns on vintage holiday music in the background while the three of us talk idly about classes and teachers. This feels so normal. I wonder why we're listening to Christmas music when Tate and his family are so clearly Jewish.

I look at Tate. "So, uh, Christmas music?"

"What? Jews don't like a little holiday spirit?"

"I didn't say that."

He smiles, nudging me with his elbow. "We're weird, I know. It's family winter tradition."

Tate gestures toward the couch, and I sit down as he eases in next to me, almost touching my body with his, his mom in a love seat catty-corner to us. I sit with my feet tucked under me, hands wrapped around the warm mug, Tate consuming the space around me. The sweet smell of chocolate and the warmth of Tate's body in his woolly sweater leaning into me is —I could close my eyes and freefall like this forever.

"So tell me more about you, Aden," Sandy says. She takes a slow sip of her cocoa, which I saw her spike with Bailey's before she sat down.

"What do you want to know?"

I'm not sure if she's putting me on the spot or if she genuinely wants to know me.

"What do you love?"

Tate. I almost say it because his name has become synonymous with love in my obsessive head, but instead I take my time. What do I love, not who.

"I love music. But you already know that. I love math, particularly calculus, but you know that, too. I don't know."

"Ade's a lover," Tate says.

I elbow him. Thanks.

"Ow. I meant that in a good way. You are. You're passionate about so many things. It's hard to pin you down. You're a lover."

I give him a sideways glance.

"That's a wonderful way to be," Sandy says. "But I would've guessed that from the moment we met. Some people are passionate in general. I'm like that, too. It's exhausting, isn't it?"

I smile. "Completely."

"What do you love?" I ask her.

"That's easy. Art."

"Maybe this is a dumb question, but why do you love art?"

Tate smiles at me and nudges my arm ever so slightly. A secret's passed between us. He likes my question, or the way I'm interacting with his mom, or the warmth of this moment.

"I love art because it's a way to express and preserve feelings that might otherwise be forever lost. When that thought or feeling or perception is expressed and interpreted by someone who experiences the art, it's made bigger than it was to begin with. And over time, art, collectively, tells us more about who we are as human beings than anything else."

"That makes perfect sense. But isn't there art in almost everything?"

Tate and Sandy exchange a look.

"Yes." Tate answers my question.

"I believe that if it's an authentic form of expression, no

matter the medium, then yes. There is art in so much that we do. But in my opinion, art is made with purpose, intent to express or communicate, if that makes sense." Tate's mom says this gently, smiling because it's assumed we speak the same language. And we do.

I think of my dad in the basement building and welding. There is art in all of that.

I could swear Tate is leaning harder than he was before, but it's slight, and I'm drowning and swirling and losing myself in this moment.

"We're gonna go to my room and hang for a bit," Tate says, hopping off the couch.

"We are?" I think that's me talking.

"Okay, sweetie," Sandy says. She gets up. "I'm heading to bed." She squeezes his arm and gives me a warm smile.

"G'night, Mom."

"Good night," I say.

Tate's room is in the basement. When we get there, he says, "Wait here. I'll be right back."

He bounds out of the room, and I sit down on his unmade bed. It smells musty, but it's Tate's must. I consider lying down, putting my head on the pillows, pulling the Tate-blankets over me. I don't. Tate returns quickly with the bottle of Bailey's his mom was using for her cocoa.

"Don't you think your mom will notice? What about your dad?"

"Nah," he says. "She rarely drinks it. And there's another full bottle of this stuff in the liquor cabinet. My dad will get home in the middle of the night or not all. And when he does get here, he's a zombie. He'll sleep into the day."

"Okay."

What does this mean? I will myself not to say anything because it might take the magic out of this moment, but if I drink here, I can't drive home.

"What?" Tate says, taking a swig of the sweet liquor straight from the bottle.

"Are you sure this is a good idea? I mean, how will I get home?" Magic broken?

"It's no problem. We'll just tell my mom we fell asleep talking. She won't ask questions. Promise."

I raise my eyebrows.

"She won't ask questions?"

"Nope. She's really cool about this kind of thing. She trusts me."

Trusts him to what? Not have sex with girls when they're alone in his bedroom all night? Not that sex is where this is going, but . . .

Tate hands me the bottle. I take a drink. It's sweet but strong, burning on the way down my throat. Then I text my dad that I'm staying at Marissa's again tonight. My insides are cringing because if I drink I'll be stuck here with Tate all night, and though it's all I want, maybe it's not all I want.

Tate turns on the Shins. "Kissing the Lipless"—our song. He grabs my hands, and we dance around the room together, free, singing at the top of our lungs. We're buried in the basement, Tate's mom on the third level. I'm hoping she can't hear us. I try not the think about the lyrics of the song—about wearing your heart on your sleeve for someone and burying a friendship.

I flop onto his bed, winded. He sits down on the floor next to the bed and leans his head back. My hair hangs off the bed next to Tate. He reaches for my hair and runs his fingers through the ends. I'm floating, present but out of control because part of me is evaporating with each slow stroke of Tate's hand in my hair. I'm not sure if we're both drunk, because the wild feelings I have for Tate are convoluting the alcohol. Or the other way around.

When we make eye contact, I know. He knows. Something at once small and huge passes between us. Then his mouth is on mine and we are kissing because, finally, *finally,* we're not fighting it or questioning it or pulling away. We are letting go together because if we don't . . . If we don't, I will die by not-kissing.

Tate's hands are on either side of my face, and he's gently pushing me backwards. I'm on my back, his body pressing into me. Our mouths together. His mouth against mine is everything a first kiss is supposed to be. It's soft and hard, earnest yet unassuming. He tastes like Bailey's and butter and salt. This kiss is saying everything he's never said. I've fallen into a black hole—lost myself in this strange mix of dark and light, and I'm not sure I'll ever recover.

We are kissing, our bodies pretzeling together. It's like we've done it a thousand times before, but it's also new and beautifully awkward. It's loving him hard and soft. It's fingertips exploring faces. It's knowing each other's depths. He traces his hand along my collarbone, and I thank God for my collarbone, a beautiful, sensual spot on my body where neck and chest converge.

He rolls on top of me and puts his hand on my stomach and then reaches around my back, pressing our bodies into each other. Everything I ever thought was true about my body just isn't. Because here in Tate's arms, his hands, I am liberated. I'm not too fat. I'm nothing that isn't enough. I'm just a spirit and a body and in that I am enough.

We vacillate between the intensity of loving each other right here and now, to laughing.

Everything is perfect except for one thing. Right in the middle of this intense joy is a piercing sadness I can't name.

***

I have no idea what time it is when I wake up, but I am alone. I'm alone in Tate's bed. I touch my face—I can feel his hands on my cheeks before he put his mouth to mine. It's like moving from sea to land. The waves are still moving my body—we're still kissing.

I listen for the sound of a flushing toilet, something to say he's coming back. That he hasn't left me alone. But somehow I knew from the moment I woke that he's not in the bathroom. He's not coming back to lie next to me and kiss again. He's gone, and I'm alone.

Something inside me breaks.

Leaving Tate's house alone and broken at five in the morning is bitter. I am a fool. I gather my things from his bedroom floor and suck in breath after sour breath, forcing the tears down into my belly.

It's not snowing anymore, but the hush of it lingers here, made loud by the sound of my mitten against the windshield as I try to deice it without a scraper.

A light comes on in Tate's house and he pulls a curtain aside. He doesn't move when I look up and spot him standing in the window watching me. He is watching me struggle with my mitten and the ice. Tears are spilling freely down my face. Tate just stands there watching. A tall, unfeeling shadow in the window.

MARISSA

*S*he's been wearing dark eyeliner all week. We are the same, me and Marissa. Both fools. Both sad and alone. Both keeping things to ourselves. We've drifted from each other.

"Just come to Ike's with me," I say as I walk by my best friend, who's staring into her empty locker.

"I thought you'd never ask."

She orders a mocha. I'm tempted to get a black coffee to even us out, but I'm not that interested in making a statement. It'll be two mochas. Extra whip.

She doesn't know about the other night with Tate. In turn there's something she's not telling me. And yet there's a comfortable understanding between us.

After I tell her about Tate, she reaches a hand across the table and places it on top of mine. She doesn't say anything, just squeezes a little. She knows about this love and this pain.

We're still holding hands when she tells me she's pregnant.

"What about the morning-after pill?"

"Yeah," she says. "I got lucky. I took it too late, or too early, or something. You know what they say, Ade. Nothing but abstinence is a hundred percent."

We're both completely numb. There's a chance this baby is Danson's. If it's not Danson's, it's Josh's. So it's Lance Danson or Josh Melling who'll be connected to Marissa for the rest of her life. Starting now.

It's my turn for silence. I stay holding her hand, but I don't squeeze. She's not ready. She's in the place where if I make a wrong move, she'll burst into tears or get mad, and she doesn't want to feel any of that right now. She shifts out of my grip and wraps both hands around her mocha.

I'm biting my tongue because it's not obvious to me what she'll do. If she'll keep it.

"I'm keeping it, Ade. I feel different. Everything is changing." And she's right. Everything is changing.

She's making a decision that will change her life in ways she doesn't even realize. She can't go back on this. I guess if she chose to abort, she couldn't go back on that either. But she wouldn't be a mother.

"Can you do something for me?" she says.

"Yes."

"Come with me when I tell my mom?"

MOMS

*S*he was beautiful once. I think having been beautiful once is Cassandra's big claim to fame. Which is shallow and sad at best. At worst it's pathetic. Cassandra's dated rich men, and she says Marissa's dad was some hotshot in a band. The truth is probably closer to Marissa's dad could be any one of the several guys she was sleeping with when she got pregnant. I don't think Cassandra has ever been as beautiful as Marissa. But Marissa's beauty is better than skin-deep. Cassandra? Now the alcohol and cigarettes have taken their toll, and she looks ten years older than she is. She's only thirty-seven. Her smile lines are deep wrinkles next to her mouth. She has puffy shadows underneath her eyes. She's a walking ashtray, and I'm not sure she sees herself as valuable at all.

She's never been to a parent-teacher conference. She brings men home from bars. I've been Marissa's best friend for ten years, and she acts like I'm a stranger. There should be a law against women like her having babies.

I think of Marissa. She'll be the exact same age as her mom when Cassandra had Alex. Maybe Marissa was screwed from the start. I wonder if a teenager could ever make a good mother.

Cassandra stands in her kitchen drinking a brown smoothie.

"The perfect cure for a mild hangover," she says. If the circles of mascara under her eyes and the stench of stale alcohol indicate a mild hangover, I'd hate to see a major one.

Marissa and I sit next to each other on the worn navy pinstriped couch. The curtains are drawn, but the "garden level" apartment doesn't pull much light anyway. *Garden* is another word for basement. It's no wonder Marissa is hardly ever here. I move to find some semblance of bodily comfort, and dust wafts up from the couch cushions. The cigarette smell is as stifling as the clutter and lack of light.

"Mom," Marissa says. Cassandra ignores her in favor of her brown smoothie and a cigarette.

"Mom," she says again, louder. "We need to talk."

"No, we don't." Cassandra's bitchy is fresh as ever. She's not making eye contact. She's staring wistfully out the window, smoking her cigarette like she's Ginger fucking Rogers. She's waiting for something better. She'll always be waiting.

"Mom, please." Suddenly I see the little girl in Marissa, and my heart breaks because Cassandra will never show up.

"I'll save you the trouble. I know you're knocked up. I'm not an idiot."

She's still standing in the kitchen smoking a cigarette and choking down that brown crap.

I want to get up and shake her, but I don't because this

is not my battle. It's Marissa's. *Your daughter is going to have a baby. You are going to be a grandmother. Shape the fuck up.* I guess some people just can't. Or won't. Marissa's mom must be afraid to really be alive. Because what would it mean for her to feel alive? I'm guessing it would mean feeling a lot of pain and regret.

I take hold of Marissa's hand and squeeze hard. *This* is what I will do. I'll love Marissa and hold her in this space that isn't toxic.

Cassandra is still standing there, unaffected, smoking and drinking. Staring out the window.

"So?" Marissa says. It's the most desperate question I've ever heard. And it's met unanswered.

We start to gather our stuff. Marissa will hang out at my house for the rest of the day. At least I love her. I can't say the same for Cassandra. This can't be love.

"Whose is it?" she says.

"That's what you want to know? Whose it is?"

"I have seventy bucks in my handbag," Cassandra says. "You can have it for the abortion."

But Cassandra knows Marissa isn't having an abortion. She'll make Marissa say it.

"I'm keeping it."

"I may've raised you to be a slut," Cassandra says. "But I didn't raise you to be an idiot. What the fuck happened to the condoms?"

"I don't know."

"No," Cassandra says. "What you don't know. What you

really don't know, is what it means to be a mother. You have no goddamned clue."

"Neither do you."

Each knife cuts sharper than the last. They match each other in low, stabbing tones. It's worse than screaming.

"You can cut me down all you want, Missy, but I'll be damned if I let you blame me for this."

Who wouldn't blame the whole of Cassandra's parenting for this?

Marissa cries the ten minutes it takes to get to my house.

When we pull into the driveway, she's wiping at her eyes with a tissue and reapplying mascara.

"Should we tell my dad?" I ask, because I'm out of ideas, and I don't know who else could possibly help her.

"Yeah," she says.

DAD

We traverse the basement stairs together. When our eyes meet, I give Marissa a soft smile. Though I'm not certain how my dad will receive this information, it can't be any worse than Cassandra's reaction.

"Dad, can we talk?"

He's wearing safety goggles. Doing something with a power tool and wood. He stops with the tool and pulls his goggles atop his head.

"What's up?" He's way too chipper for the shit about to hit the fan.

"Upstairs?"

He casts a glance at me and then at Marissa. He knows this is weird.

"Yeah. Give me five minutes. I'll meet you on the porch."

We walk back up the stairs, both of us in shock. Moving around the kitchen together wordlessly, we brew some coffee. She finds the filters—I get the coffee and the creamer. We move to turn the brewer on at the same time, giggling a little as our hands clash. Side by side, we lean into the kitchen counter, listening to the soothing steam and drip of the coffeemaker.

My dad joins us on the porch with a cup of his own, none of the three of us eager to start the discussion.

Finally, I turn to Marissa, a question on my face, asking if I can say it. She nods, and I say it out loud for the first time. To my father. My best friend is pregnant. When he comes to, after the shock of it, my dad asks the obvious, "Are you keeping it?"

"Yes."

Her resolution is still jolting. *Yes.* She is having a baby.

I don't know how it happened, but I look up and the two of them are standing, and my dad is holding Marissa, and she's crying again. It's a side-hug, her face buried in his shirt. He is the dad she needs right now, and my heart breaks double because I'm not sure what, if anything, he can do for Marissa. And because I've never been sure when I can count on my dad's warm dadness. I'm grateful it's now, for Marissa. But I also know he's doing this for me, too.

I look at the two of them in their side-embrace, and I think we all know that this moment is not a promise. She could use a promise. I wish so much that Cassandra could've shown up for even one minute.

JON

When he finds out Marissa's pregnant, he sits down clutching his stomach like the wind has been knocked out of him. Like he's me and he's just seen Tate and Maggie making out.

I forgot that he'd have a reaction to this.

"Whose is it?"

"Marissa's."

It's the best answer I can find.

"I guess it doesn't matter," he says. "I knew she had issues, but this?"

"I know."

I agree with him, and silently thank the powers that be that it isn't his. And then I feel guilty because it's hers.

"She's keeping it?"

"I wouldn't be telling you if she wasn't. She wanted me to tell you. She has enough on her plate."

"Wow."

Jon looks up at me through his little-boy self.

I sit down next to him.

"I feel so bad for her," he says. "How did the three of us end up such messes?"

"Speak for yourself." But he's right. We're all carrying something.

I put my arm around my brother's shoulder and lean my head into his.

ME

J love the word *joy* because it sounds exactly as it feels. It starts with a consonant and ends in a rich deep vowel. Joy couldn't mean anything other than what it means.

I felt joy as a child, when my mom was alive. And I've felt it with Tate. And with Marissa, when we're laughing or crazy, when we just don't care what other people think. And with Jon.

The drive doesn't start with anything resembling joy. It starts heavy, thick with self-pity. It starts with a head full of Marissa, and Tate, and Jon, and my dad. It starts with Seth Bernum and the residue of burning shame. It starts motherless and unloved.

Tate's not here. I can't be with him after we did whatever we did with our souls and bodies that night. Because now, after everything, being with Tate isn't freeing. It's oppressive. I think of the way he brushes past my desk in calculus. The way he takes up so much space in a room, in me. I need to get away.

And so I do. With one hand on the steering wheel and

the other on the stick shift, I shove the car into first and then second and then third gear, each rev of the engine, each turn of the wheel, in my control.

I choose my music and roll down the windows in spite of the piercingly cold air and speed out of town on a dirt road —not the one Tate and I usually drive. This road is different: it's mine.

Flashes of Tate—his glow, his kiss, his essence—haunt me until I imagine the wind pushing him out and away; it's like letting go of the string attached to a balloon. It's an epiphany that he can't love me in the way I need.

Even my mom, my dad, my brother, they come to mind, but I can't hold them all here with me. It's just too crowded and heavy. So I let the wind take them away, too. And Danson, and Marissa.

Until I'm alone with myself and the music and the wind. I'm just . . . present. Breathing the wind. Sunshine on my skin. Road beneath me.

And so if only momentarily, I free myself, and I feel . . . joy.

ME

I lie on my bed alone, forcing myself to go two minutes, then five, then back to two without looking at my phone. Without checking social media for Tate or Maggie or both. I'm forcing myself not to text him. Because loving him and letting him touch me, hold my hand, stroke my hair, but knowing I'm not supposed to interpret it *like that*, even though we light the air on fire—it's too painful.

I need to leave my room. And my phone. So I grab my car keys and my wallet, no phone. I drive to the grocery store but sit in my car staring at the gym next door. I thought I saw something in the paper a few months ago that they have a pool, but the place looks way too small for that. The sign on the door reads COME IN!

I walk by the door twice without going inside. I want to enter. This could be the start of something. It's just a gym nestled in a strip mall next to a grocery store. But it's a gym. I haven't done anything gymlike in forever. I'm not sure my body remembers how to do anything gymlike.

I extend my hand and place it on the door handle, pulling the door open. It's now or never.

Inside, it's a little cramped and there's so much equipment. I wouldn't know the first thing about any of this. I sigh and consider leaving. But I'm here. And so I will explore what there is.

A hand on my shoulder. I turn around, and I look into translucent blue eyes the color of the ocean when you can see all the way to the bottom. The eyes turn up in a smile, and I see a boy a little older than me attached to the eyes. I think about leaving again, but there's something warm about him, about this place. So I don't leave.

"You're not a regular." It's a statement. His voice is soft, warm, and wow, I can see all the way to the sand at the bottom of his eyes.

"This is my first time."

He extends a hand. A big hand. "Dustin. Can I show you around?"

"Please."

Dustin shows me the equipment, and it's all I can do to pay attention to what he's saying. I'm disappointed because I don't see the pool.

"Obviously you don't have a pool?"

"Oh, but we do. Only the awesomest pool in town. It's on the roof."

"The roof?"

"It's four lanes. Kept around seventy-eight degrees and

open all year round unless the weather is extreme—then we have to keep the cover on."

"Wow," I say. "That *is* pretty awesome."

"The stairs are in the women's locker room. I'd show you that, too, but I'm not sure the other ladies would appreciate it. I'll meet you on the pool deck. Steam and sauna in the locker room, too. It's nice after a swim."

He's right about that.

We meet on the deck, and there's an open lane. I feel like tearing my clothes off and jumping in now. Ripples of aquamarine, steam rising from the surface, and it's quiet save two lap swimmers who don't look much faster than me. The chlorine burns my nose a little, reminding me of hours spent playing in the pool with my brother when we were kids. My mom loved swimming, too.

A woman in a swishy neon warm-up suit right out of 1989 walks over to us.

"Hi," she says. Her voice is gruff, but she seems nice enough. "Is Dustin here giving you the tour of the gym?"

"Yeah," I say. "It's nice."

"Built it from the ground up."

"You're the owner?"

"Nancy Dillon. Nice to meet you."

Nancy must be in her late fifties, but she clearly takes care of her body. I suppose that's no surprise, given she owns a gym.

"You a swimmer?"

"Kinda."

"Kinda?" she says. "You either are or you aren't."

"I love swimming. I know my strokes. But I haven't been in the water for a few years."

"Well, you've come to the right place. Swimming is my passion. When I was young I was assistant coach for Team USA. Spent seven good years coaching Olympians. Used to coach it over at the high school, too, but after I opened this joint, just didn't have the time for it anymore. You should try our masters swim."

I'm out of my league here. I can't swim for a former Olympic coach. I can't even swim for a high school coach. I'm not varsity material. I'm not workout material. This was a mistake.

"You got plans the next hour?" Nancy says.

"I'm sorry?"

"My class starts in ten. You can join us."

"Oh," I say. "I don't have my suit. And I might need to swim a few laps before I join the masters."

"Nonsense," she says. "Dustin, get her outfitted in one of the lost and found suits and find a pair of goggles. Don't worry, we launder everything. And we split up by pace and ability. We'll start you in the slow lane. We've got a pregnant mom and an eighty-eight-year-old in that lane. You'll be just fine. Now, you have seven minutes. Go."

Nancy is brusque and bossy, but there's something kind about the way she immediately decides to push me. Like she's taking me under her wing.

Mercifully, Dustin finds a suit that fits me, and I'm relieved that I can head upstairs without having to parade through the main part of the gym in the borrowed suit. It's a bit old-ladyish, but modest, and I like the way it looks on my body. I don't have time to inspect my image in the mirror for too long.

I also don't have time to lower gently into the pool, because Nancy's got everyone warming up, and she's motioning me to my lane with arms waving wildly. Wow, she's really into this.

The water is frigid, and I'm glad to start moving right away. The shock of cold as body joins water in movement wakes me.

Nancy takes no prisoners. The workout kicks my butt, and I can barely finish the modified version of the drills. By the last set, everyone, including the old man and pregnant lady, is done with their workouts, but they are all crowded at the end of my lane to cheer me on.

"How many more laps?" Nancy yells as I pull water, getting ready to flip-turn and start another lap. I stick my hand out of the water and sign *two*. I can hear the dull roar of the class and Nancy cheering as I flip-turn and make my way back to them. I'm high. High and exhausted and, I think, proud.

I'm halfway through the last lap, leaving my classmates at the other end of the pool cheering me on. It's just me now. The water slicks down my body as I move through it. Water rushes off my face as I turn my head and gasp for air. I'm lost in the rhythm of body, mind, soul, pushing and pulling, kicking, struggling to finish. But I will. I will finish this lap.

I climb out of the pool, and Nancy tosses a towel at me. I nod my thanks. I'm not cold like I should be, soaking wet in thirty-eight degrees. I'm hot from the exertion.

"Three times a week," Nancy says. "Monday, Wednesday, and Friday."

"I can do that, but I need to talk to my dad about membership cost," I say.

"You got a job?"

"No."

"No?" she says. Is she judging me?

"School," I say. "I'm a school geek, so between studying and choir, I haven't had much time."

"Oh, well, I was going to offer you a work trade, but if you don't have time . . ."

"That's nice. I mean I might have time now. I'm a senior so it's a little different than last year. What kind of time commitment?"

"Six hours a week at the front desk, greeting members and touring walk-ins, wiping down equipment once an hour in exchange for your membership. You can do it in one shift or two. We'll have to look at the schedule, but Saturday evenings are hard to fill."

"I can do a six-hour shift on Saturdays. No problem."

What else would I be doing besides wallowing in Marissa's pregnancy or reviewing math homework I've already completed?

"Done, then," she says. "But you're here three times a week for masters, no exceptions. It's part of your work-trade commitment, got it?"

"Yes. Thank you so much."

I wonder how Nancy can just hire me like that without knowing the first thing about me. I wonder how she can be so bossy about me getting to her masters class. But I find myself accepting her challenge, wanting to be there, swimming regularly, losing myself in the water and the exertion. I must need this.

When I come out of the locker room, Dustin is standing bent over the front desk reading a document. I can't help but admire the definition in his biceps, the angles of his jawline.

He catches me staring and looks up. There's something behind his smile, and I'm not sure if it's arrogance or if he's teasing me, but I am curious.

I shrug and realize I don't care that he knows I'm staring. I walk out without saying anything, but I think I've said a lot. I can't help myself. I glance back to see if he's watching me. He's still looking through the glass doors. He smiles half at me and half to himself, and returns to his document shaking his head.

Dustin. It's a good name. Like Aden.

JON

*L*et's drive."

We're on our way home from school, the weather is crap, but I don't want to be home yet. Isolated in our rooms.

"Only if there's licorice involved," Jon says.

"You've got yourself a deal."

We stop at the closest gas station and load up on licorice and pop.

We agree on rap and '60s rock as our soundtrack. I drive. He eats. Licorice stick after licorice stick.

"So what did your coach say?"

"He knows they dropped the possession charges, so he said I can work out with the team and practice minimally. But the team can't practice with me too much, because it's hard and fast that I won't be playing any games this year. And he'll appeal to the dean about next year."

"What do you think?"

He inhales through his nose, finishing a bright red stick before he says, "I asked the coach for a week off because, honestly, Ade, I might take the rest of the year off."

"What about the scholarship?" I think of Brandeis and Boston and how badly I need to leave. Maybe it's the last time I'll contribute to the pressure on Jon, but I need to know.

Jon looks up at me, "I think I need to see if I can get into RISD."

My face falls, but I catch myself and smile at him. My little brother. For a second, I see his five-year-old self, dressed in nothing but undies and a cape sitting next to me.

"I have to try, Ade."

"I know you do." We all do.

SABITA

Beauty. I've been wrong about it for a long time. I thought it was something to achieve. A destination. But I can't aspire to be beautiful because it's not about getting there —it's about being there.

The art studio is right across the hall from the choir room. Stools and chairs and countertops made of various materials clutter the room. A soft winter light pours from skylights and windows onto half-done paintings, sculptures, and blown glass. The space is perfectly suited for creation.

Sabita leans into a patch of light from a window on the far side of the room. She's elbow-deep in wet clay. Hair tied back, but a few wispy strands fall around her face. Her brow is pinched in deep concentration. Music plays on an antiquated boom box sitting on the counter next to her.

She makes eye contact with me briefly. Her eyes relax into a momentary smile but not long enough for her mouth to catch up. She's working intently. She moves left, and I see what she's molding. It's the face of an elephant. So far, half the face of an elephant. Each intricate feature of the elephant's face from wrinkle to rough, weatherworn skin is crafted. Such that she, the elephant, is real. She has depth and character. I've never seen anything like it. And it's in the depth and breadth of the elephant's half face that I finally see Sabita without the filter I've been using all this time. I see that she's more than her physical beauty, that she's more than Jon's girlfriend. She's an artist. She's a full person.

I give Sabita a small wave and back out of the room. She's supposed to meet me and Jon on the lacrosse field in fifteen minutes to drive home for dinner. I plop down on the floor in the hall and grab my ten-pound history book. I'll wait for her here.

We walk to the field together, and I find myself telling her about the new gym and swimming.

"Wow, Ade. That is so cool. I'm so happy for you." And she genuinely is happy for me.

I sigh because I get it. Sabita is as beautiful as she is radiant. She's warm in the way kindness and compassion are warm, enveloping. She's light in the way excitement and laughter are light. She's cute in the way a child experiences the world as new. And I realize that perhaps my fascination with her borders the crush line, but mostly I just want to be a little more like her. A little more childlike and open. I want to be. A little more beautiful. A little more radiant.

And I can be.

I am.

I have to go through my dad's closet to get into the attic. In the past we haven't been allowed up here. Probably more a safety issue than a privacy issue. At least I hope that's the case, because I'm already crawling through pink insulation. I wonder if it's bad to inhale this stuff.

None of the boxes are labeled, and it takes me twenty minutes to find the clothes. I knew we had some boxes, but I had no idea my dad or mom saved every last piece of baby garment we ever wore. So many footie pajamas.

I pull matching pajamas out of the box, one blue, one pink. Terry cloth. I find T-shirts and shorts, mini one-piece body suits. I smile, thinking of a childhood in these clothes with an alive mom.

Marissa won't have to spend much on clothing, at least for the first few years.

I decide to keep the terry cloth footies because they've been so well loved. And Jon and I must've been so well loved in them.

I discover the USB sticks inside a shoebox inside another

box. Despite my mom's aversion to labeling, the USB sticks each have a small sticky note in my mom's handwriting taped to the outside that reads *Family photos*. The sticks are buried under a few random prints. In one of the prints, my mom stands in the woods, having found the perfect patch of light. I stare at the picture for a long time, wishing I could jump inside it. My mom is love embodied—it's in the way she smiles at the camera, or whoever's taking the picture.

I throw the USB sticks and a stack of prints inside one of the big boxes of baby clothes, and the plan forms as I climb down the ladder.

It takes me three hours to pick out the pictures. I need the perfect balance. Some of all of us. Some of just her and Dad. Some of just her and Jon, just her and me. Just Dad and Jon, just Dad and me. I choose several prints from the pile, and more off the USB. I'll need ten frames for all the prints.

I love the one of just her. She's under a tree, and the camera is zoomed in on her face, the yellowing autumn aspen leaves blurred in the background. Her beautiful, youthful, healthy face. It's a face with so much ahead of it. So much possibility. I'd like to believe she did live, if not a full life, then full moments, full days beyond when this picture was taken. I have to believe it. Otherwise what a waste.

I'm lucky. The project costs me seventy-five dollars total, and it's all the cash I have. I need to babysit again.

I hang framed pictures on the wall where the holes are. I prop them on the mantel near the fireplace. And I keep the one of just mom. It's on my desk.

I miss my dad on Saturday after the pictures are hung. I work my first shift at the gym, and then Marissa comes over to watch a movie in the basement, where we crash. I wake up early, leaving Marissa downstairs. She's been sleeping a lot.

I creep up the stairs, afraid all of my pictures will have been taken down.

I smell the deep smoke of morning coffee, hear the *glub-glub* of our ancient Mr. Coffee brewer. Dad is sitting at the kitchen table, his hands wrapped around his mug. SUPER DAD. The mug from which he drinks his coffee religiously. He's staring at the family collage I made and hung on the wall in the breakfast nook. Dad and Mom at their wedding, a family shot at Disneyland, and one of us camping.

I stand motionless next to the kitchen counter. My dad's back is turned as he pours himself a cup of fresh coffee.

His back still to me, having sensed my presence, he says, "Did you hang the photographs, Aden?" He sounds brusque, on the brink of angry.

"I did." I stand there in my skin, wishing he would turn around and face me, face *it*. "You sound mad."

He puts both hands on the counter, leaning over the steaming cup of coffee, a pose that makes his body look so heavy. Still, he refuses to look at me.

"I was."

"Mad?"

He angles his body, raises his head, our eyes meet—two faces that look alike. "After ten years, it still hurts to see her face without warning." The tears well in him, a tear for each eye.

My own eyes widen.

I consider saying *I'm sorry* because I don't want to cause him any more pain, but I think better of it. It's time to be done protecting each other. The way he imagines he protects me from his anguish, the way I avoid talking about her and keep the cycle going. So, instead of *I'm sorry*, I say, "I miss her too."

And I stand in the kitchen with my dad while he deals with the discomfort of our collective grief.

He speaks first. "Your mom made us go on that trip." He taps the photo from Disneyland. "I'm pretty sure she gave me an ultimatum; she wanted to take the two of you so badly. She wasn't always a saint, your mom. She was outspoken and bossy. My God, she was bossy." He takes a drink of steaming coffee, and I stay as still as possible, not moving a muscle for fear of breaking this spell.

"So we walk in the gates and there's Belle from *Beauty and the Beast* standing right there. Jon was four. But he'd seen the movie. He was so wildly excited he literally started running circles around Belle. And your jaw. It was on the floor. At the sight of you two, so happy, so innocently and just wildly happy and excited, your mom just lost it. She started laughing and crying. Happy tears.

"Nothing made us happier than you and Jon. Nothing. We shared a whole world, your mom and I. And I'm not saying we stayed together because of you two. I'm saying we stayed in love because of you two."

That's the most I've ever heard my dad speak about my mom, and momentarily, I'm a little girl listening to my dad tell a deeply satisfying story. Hearing about my mom fills me.

My dad grunts his goodbye and leaves the kitchen.

I quietly pour myself a cup of coffee and sit down so I can stare at the photographs of my young mom. This time, the pictures stay.

*H*e's been making a show of his relationship with Maggie lately. Lots of hallway handholds and kissing. The kissing is still a swift and hard punch in the gut. But maybe they've always been this way and I'm just noticing more. I hate noticing, because I'm trying so hard not to love him. I wonder how he can know so much of me, hold so much of me, without loving me enough to be with me? Maybe he just loves Maggie more. If I think about it too long, I feel unlovable. But I've already resolved to embody beauty. So I am washing feelings of unlove away every time they assault me, letting them roll over, around, and off of me.

I suck in a breath because I have to pass them as a couple to get to my next class. And I'll be damned if TateandMaggie will make me late.

"Ade." It's Tate saying my name. I half turn and keep walking forward. I don't want to talk to him, and where I used to love the sound of his voice saying *Ade* with a loving familiarity, today it makes me want to kick him. Where does he get off?

"Hey, Tate," I say. Maybe that's enough. Just a hi in the hallway.

I'm walking fast, and it takes Tate all of two giant steps before he's in stride with me, Maggie heading in the opposite direction to class.

"What's up?" The way he says it makes me feel pathetic. It's laced with pity and condescending gentleness. It's been three weeks since our night together. I've been making up excuses as to why I can't hang out. Even though every text, every invasion of space when he walks by my desk or smiles brightly, says he expects me to act the same with him. As though we weren't recklessly in love, if only for one night.

"Nothing," I say.

"Not nothing," he says.

He thinks he can call me on my evasion of him. Like if he makes our night together and me loving him mine alone, then *we* can still be in spite of it. Like we've been all this time. But I know *we* can't be. Because *I* can't be. I can't be part of his *we*. The *we* that isn't enough, that leaves me feeling help-less and barely loved and ultimately cheap. No. I can't be part of Tate's *we*.

"Please, Ade. Come to Ike's with me." The way he says it. *Come to Ike's with me.* It pulls on me because all I want to do, body and soul, is be with him, and he can't or won't be with me. Yes. I could go to Ike's with him. And pretend noth-ing ever happened. Pretend we haven't kissed. Pretend I don't love him and he doesn't know, and we could just be like that together for who knows how long. Even though he holds my hand and strokes my hair every time we're alone. Even though he leans into me, his body drawn to mine because our souls just get each other. Even though we let go together one night. I can't pretend that I'm okay with him because I can't be as we were . . . something more than friends, something less than lovers. It costs too much.

I have to stop.

"I can't, Tate." For a split second I think I see hurt in his eyes, but I can't acknowledge it, let alone embrace it or let it be my responsibility.

"I have swimming."

But that's not entirely honest.

"Swimming?"

The way he says it. As though he has any right to be surprised about the newness I've brought into my life.

"Yeah, and I really have to go because I'm, like, five minutes late for class now."

The bobby pins securing the yarmulke to his hair glint under the light.

"Maybe tomorrow?"

His persistence is alarming, and again I wonder why. Or how. How can he act like he hasn't inhaled me and kissed me and loved me? How can he act like I haven't poured myself into loving him? How can he take so much from me and then go back to Maggie?

"Why? I mean, how can I?"

"What do you mean why or how?" he says. "You just do. You come to Ike's with me."

He can't be honest. With me. With himself. Or if he is being honest, then I can't meet him at Ike's or wherever the hell else he is, because it will never be that simple for me.

"I can't pretend that we didn't make out, Tate. I can't pretend that I don't want more every time you hold my hand or play with my hair. Every time we make eye contact or share some inside joke. I can't just let that slide like it doesn't mean more to me than friendship. I just can't be that person for you. It's like . . . you're leading me on or something. And, it just . . . It takes too much out of me." The truth is painful and liberating all at once, a rush. Because if I don't start saying my truth aloud, if I don't start living it, I will burn from the inside out, ashes left in my wake.

He stops in his tracks, and I move forward. Maybe he's shocked or hurt or both. But I have to keep walking. I'm late.

MARISSA

*T*wo months later.

I hand Marissa two sticks of green spearmint gum. She unwraps both sticks and shoves them into her mouth with a moan. She hasn't stopped complaining about the nausea for the last two weeks. She's been borrowing clothes from me. I'm trying not to let the clothes-borrowing mess with my body image, because before the pregnancy Marissa was in a lot of size zeros. And she can't afford a whole new maternity wardrobe. My tunics are particularly cute with her little bump poking out of her unbuttoned jeans.

Marissa tosses a magazine onto the end table.

"I hate kids," she says after watching a pregnant mom drag her screaming toddler back to the examination room.

"Wow," I say. "That's comforting to hear from a future mother."

"I didn't say I'd hate my own. But definitely other people's brats. Can't stand 'em."

The nurse calls us to the exam room. I planned on waiting outside, but Marissa forces me to accompany her. I want to remind her that I'll be out of state next year. I can't be her person. We need to talk about it. But not now. Right now I'm here.

"They are trying to destroy my nipples," she says adjusting the hospital gown while she sits on the exam table.

She's holding the paper away from her breasts. Marissa says she wasn't expecting her boob changes. The nausea and belly growth, sure. But that her boobs have taken on a life of their own has been a very unwelcome shock, as she really did have wonderful breasts.

The tech knocks on the door and enters the room. She's all business, wheeling the ultrasound machine over to the bedside and flipping the switch.

"Are we finding out the sex of the baby today?"

"I'm sorry?" says Marissa.

"Are we finding out the sex of the baby?"

"I didn't know we could do that. I mean, I didn't know we could do that today."

The tech looks at her watch.

"We should be able to do that today," the tech says. "You're seventeen weeks. There's no guarantee at this stage, given the age of the fetus and the positioning, but there is a strong chance we will see the boy or girl parts. So, would you like to know?"

"Well, obviously," Marissa says. "Yes."

The tech applies goop to Marissa's belly and uses the machine to spread it around.

"That's your baby."

Wow. It really does look like a baby. There's a real baby in there. I was expecting something resembling a peanut, but what I'm looking at is unquestionably a baby.

The tech points to the screen and angles it toward Marissa.

"Congratulations," she says. "It's a boy."

Marissa wipes tears from her eyes, and I squeeze her hand. Knowing the sex of the baby makes this one step closer to real.

Marissa told Danson and Josh the truth. That she'd slept with two people in the same time frame and she wasn't sure whose baby it was.

Josh called her a slut and hasn't spoken to her since. Funny how you think you've got someone pegged and they turn out to be the complete opposite. I thought Josh was a good guy.

Danson was surprising. He told his wife and agreed to a paternity test, the results of which return in ten to fourteen days. If it's his, he'll show up. I guess he and his wife are going to work it out, though I can't imagine how she can forgive the sleazebag for sleeping with a student. Apparently everyone's decided to keep the whole affair hush-hush, and after Marissa graduates they can sort out the details. I hope it's his, because Marissa could use all the support she can get.

But she said even if it's Josh's, she won't roll over without a fight. She'll tell his mom that she has a grandson. Marissa says Josh's mom is *good people* and his family is totally loaded. I hope that's true. The good people part.

The pregnancy seems to have changed Marissa. I've never seen her with a purpose. I'm weirdly less worried about her now than I was before she got pregnant. She got her acceptance letter from Metro State University last week. Since then, she's spent a lot less time with celeb magazines while lying on my bed after school. She's either sleeping or working on homework. She saw the school counselor and found out that Metro has a "young moms' house" affiliate off campus. I guess all the girls in the house have babies, and if you go to school and have a job, you can live there all four years and get childcare.

I don't want to leave Marissa. It kills me that I can't be the one to take care of her. But we both know I can't.

ME

My dad took us all out for ice cream to celebrate my early acceptance to Brandeis. Though I could see some of her sadness, Marissa looked truly happy for me that night. And she actually ate her entire container of ice cream.

Dad has said we'll figure it out—two private schools, one family—but Jon and I both feel the undercurrent of his worry.

I stare at the scholarship applications open in my web browser—one for women in math and science, and one for students with a deceased parent.

I start to write the essay for the deceased-parent scholarship, but how can I put words to having lost my mom to cancer and what it's been like to be me without her? Music keeps filling my head. Melodies and lyrics, the strum of a guitar. So I decide to send song lyrics and a video of me performing them as my "essay."

I flop onto my bed and look at the twelve-string guitar propped against my nightstand. I think of my mom, the word *proud* on the tip of my tongue.

*J*t's her birthday. In the past we've avoided talking about it because it hurts. Usually, the only noticeable thing about my mom's birthday is that my dad disappears. And then we keep on living like her birthday never came and went. Like *she* never came and went. But she did, and I'm here because of it. And Jon's here because of it. And this is what life looks like because my mom came and went.

Jon and I walk into the house, and see the note: *JON AND ADEN come downstairs.*

We look at each other, eyebrows raised, a question passing between us as we make our way to the basement.

When my eyes adjust to the dark, I see our dad standing with the remote in his hand.

He grumbles, motioning for us to sit.

Wow, there is a lot of popcorn. Two giant bowls of it and a few fun-size candy bars on the coffee table.

"I, uh." It takes a minute for him to collect his thoughts and words. He clears his throat. "The pictures had me

wondering what else was in the attic. I found another box."
He doesn't acknowledge the birthday, but we all know.

Without saying more, he presses a button on the remote, and there's my mom, alive and well on the screen, holding the hand of a toddler as she walks. It's me. Me and my mom. Her hair is dark and wild, just like mine. In the next clip there's Jon as a baby, playing in an empty diaper box. My mom is laughing. It's nothing like my laugh. It's this mix of flute and trombone and singing soprano. Robust. Beautiful, if slightly grating. I remember the singing soprano — but the depth and breadth of her laugh, of her person, it was lost to me. Dad was right, she is kind of loud and bossy. And funny. I don't remember that about her.

There is so much live footage of my mom. I've never seen any of this.

We're three sitting on the couch together watching the family we once were. It hurts, but it's the best kind of hurt I've had about her since she died. It's like my dad has somehow made it all real. That she existed. That she left. That it hurts. It wasn't real until now. It occurs to me that even if she were still alive, we wouldn't be that family anymore. Things are always changing; time changes everything.

I lean into my dad's sweatshirt and wipe my tears.

After, when we're eating the candy that was on the table, I announce, "I'm going to get involved at the synagogue until I leave for Brandeis."

They both look at me, surprised, and I explain that I've been in touch with Rabbi Morrey. Knowing him and knowing more about Judaism connects me to her. I need that. Because knowing her better helps me know myself.

"This is the way she would've wanted it all along." My dad's voice is tinged with regret. "I just couldn't . . ."

He trails off, and Jon and I exchange a look. But this time, we don't try to make it okay or rescue him from the truth.

Jon says, "I don't remember her voice sounding so . . ."

"Unsettling?" I offer.

"Kind of, yeah. She sounds a little sharp."

We laugh, even my dad.

"The voice of a singer," I add.

"Like you." There's a longing in Jon's voice that I recognize because it mirrors my own. It occurs to me that maybe he's envious of the way I've found our mom—through the rabbi and even before that, through song. In the same way Jon has been a barricade between Dad and me, maybe I've been a barricade between him and Mom.

"Do you want to come with me sometime?"

"Where? To temple?"

"Why not?"

Jon looks from me to Dad as if asking permission. Dad shrugs. "Dad, do you want to come?"

"I think I'll leave you guys to it."

"Yeah, I think I do," Jon says. Dad and Jon exhale in unison, and Jon chuckles before he breaks the silence. "I didn't realize how badly I needed to see her."

I know exactly what he means.

ME

The Colorado sky is an explosion of orangey pinks and blackish blues as I pull into the strip mall parking lot. A ceremonious display of beauty in a moment I wouldn't have noted otherwise. I turn off the car engine and let the music play while I stare at the sky. I have five minutes, and I'll take them.

There's a knock on my window. Three minutes into my five. I turn to see Dustin. He points at the sky, and I nod in agreement.

"What are you up to?" I say as I make my way out of the car precisely one minute earlier than I'd planned. I'm trying to decide if he's worth it.

"I have two clients and then I'll work out myself," he says.

I know he has two clients on Saturday evenings because I see him training every Saturday. He laughs a lot with his clients. But when it's go time, he pushes hard. He's a good coach. He seems like a good guy. I try not to think about Dustin too often, because I can't go through another Tate. Dustin's warm eyes and infectious laugh are noise in the background, except when I'm near him. When we're in the same room, I don't care that Tate crushed me. When we're in the same room, it's easy laughing and light blue eyes. It's brushes on the shoulder or hands touching, and I wonder, *Was that an accident?* But I know it wasn't. This is flirting.

When we're not together, I wonder how Dustin could want me. And then I let the insecurity wash away, because how could he not?

Maybe it's my body in the water day after day, or the sheer movement, or the ritual of coming here, or Nancy or Dustin, but something in me transforms a little every time I walk in the door and walk back out. I think it's all of it. This transformation—it's like I've finally found a way to anchor my body to my soul. So to say that I'm losing weight and feeling better is wrong. It's just that I've finally found a way to be more fully me. Not all the time. But enough of the time. For now.

I'm walking on the treadmill when Dustin comes to my side, sweating and breathing heavily. He pushes two buttons twice, and now I'm half jogging up a hill.

"Go harder," he says. "You're tougher than you think."

So I do. Not because he tells me to, but because I know he's right. I am.

I stare at my reflection in the locker room mirror for a long time after my workout. I threw off my T-shirt while I was on the treadmill—something new; it was hot, and I have nothing of myself to hide. Now I know what they mean when the say life is too short. What I see isn't perfect, but it's mine. And as I look at myself, I think, *I look beautiful because I'm strong*.

ME

I've fixed the broken D on my mom's twelve-string, and I'm ready to play it, not just in my room, but at Ike's. I can't see my dad, Jon, Marissa, or Sabita as I get ready for my last song. The one I wrote. But I don't need to see them right now. They're here. Mostly, though, I'm here. Out of my head and here in the room with the people who came to see me play. I'm ready to let them see me, because right now, and always, I have something to give. Freely.

> *It's in the push and pull*
> *It's in the pain and joy*
> *It's in opening up*
>
> *Love is the knowing of souls*
> *And even when it's not perfect*
> *It might be*
> *Enough*
>
> *Because I am*

Enough
And so are you

It's in the push and pull
It's in the pain and joy
It's in opening up

So be beautiful
And love with abandon
Because as far as we know
This
Is it

It's in the push and pull
It's in the pain and the joy
It's in opening up

So open up
And be free
Because as far as we know
This
Is it

This is it.

ACKNOWLEDGMENTS

And now I get to gush about all the people who've helped me along the way.

I owe a huge debt of gratitude to my talented, articulate, warm, and brilliant agent, Renee Nyen. Thank you, Renee, for your keen editorial insights, for holding fast to the soul of this book, and for just being the kind of person who *gets it*. Words fail me. I've loved being on this journey with you and knew from our first conversation that you were the agent for me. I got so, so lucky that you felt the same way about *Calculus* and me.

I am grateful to my editor, Anne Hoppe. Anne, I've been amazed by your editing wizardry, and your ability to deliver insights with so much respect for the artistry and heart of the work. I am beyond grateful to you for having absolutely pored over every detail, theme, character, and storyline in this book. Thank you for giving *Calculus* (and me) a chance to live up to its potential. I have loved working with and learning from you and consider myself insanely fortunate for having had this opportunity.

Thank you to Christine Kettner for a gorgeous design and cover; to my meticulous copy editor, Ana Deboo; to publicist Tara Sonin; and everyone at Clarion who touched this book and made it real.

I would not be the writer I am, nor would this be the book it is, without the unwavering support and insight of Robert Gatewood. RPG, I am indebted to you—your belief in me, in this book, and in the ones to follow. You see writers as they could be *and* as they are. You work tirelessly to support and uplift. Your capacity to understand the core of a manuscript but break it down and make it better is unmatched. And you do it all so carefully and respectfully. The community that you've created at the Boulder Writing Studio is a true stronghold, and I'm glad you built it and glad I found it. Your mentorship, vision, and smart-assery are a light in the dark. *Thank you* is the most inadequate phrase.

I am overflowing with gratitude for the support of my dear, dear friends and writing comrades at BWS—most of whom have known this book since it was an infant. In no particular order: Mark, Tom, Laura, Suzanne, Shannon, Chris, Alicia, Arlee. Words can't capture the depth of some of these friendships and the admiration I have for each of you as writers. Thank you for being my people. Thank you for your rich, perceptive feedback. I am a better writer because of you. Suzanne—for being one of the best friends I could never deserve. I love you so much.

Thank you to Anne Marie O'Brien and all my friends in Anne's class at Stanford. Anne, you introduced me to so many influential YA authors. Fifty pages in, I put this book in first person because of you all, and that was so right.

To my brother, Ben. How can I articulate what your support means to me? Thank you for believing in me, and pushing me, and hearing every neurotic thought I've ever had about myself as writer. Thank you for knowing that I am a writer in spite of myself. I am so glad I got to grow up with you, and that you are one of my very best friends, and that I get to call you my brother. I am so proud of the man you are—passionate, calculated, funny, articulate, and brilliant, to name a few qualities. And to my lovely and bright-and-shining sister-in-law, Laura. You are the most humbly amazing woman. Thank you for giving this book a read in its middle stages—you made it better.

To my sister and dear friend, Laura, for supporting me through leaps and bounds, mistakes and triumphs.

To my mom and dad for loving me and dealing with me and always being proud of me. Now that I'm a parent, I think I can understand what it's meant for you to love and support me all these years. I love you both so much and am so, so grateful that I got you as my guides. Mom, you are the very embodiment of love and integrity, and it shows in everything you do. I will always hold in my heart how much you love me and let it guide me. Dad, you have always seen and honored all the sides of me, even if those sides are dark or rebellious or stubborn—thank you for holding space for me in the dark and the light. I know you've given so much to being a dad.

I want to thank my generous and loving in-laws for watching my children on countless occasions while I wrote, and for just being great and tremendously helpful.

I want to thank the many pockets of friends who support me in life and life's endeavors—you know who you are, and I can only hope you know how much I appreciate you.

I want to thank my high school English teachers who turned me on to reading and writing and taught me how to do it better—Mr. Foster, Mr. Feld, Mr. Kascht.

Last but most, Dennis. Because only the two of us really know all that's gone into writing this book. I've always wanted to write this—thank you not only for supporting, but in many ways enabling, this dream come true. I know it's impacted us and our family every step of the way. You never, for one second, questioned the legitimacy of this endeavor or its importance to me. Your support is the single most important thing that made this happen. I am forever grateful to you, and I love you.

Zeke and Sage—because you've shared me with this book. Because you've made me a more whole and honest person. Because my love for each of you is its own universe.

Jessie Hilb holds a B.A. in English literature and a master's degree in social work. She lives with her family and ever-loyal herding dog in Boulder, Colorado, where she constantly reinvents herself. This is her first novel. Visit her online at www.jessiehilb.com and on Twitter: @JessieHilb.